DUKING IT OUT

ROYAL
POWERS

E.J. Russell

Cover art: Fern Lee
Edited by Meg DesCamp

ISBN: 978-1-947033-21-4

First edition
July 2020

Contact information:
ejr@ejrussell.com

DUKING IT OUT

ROYAL
POWERS

E.J. Russell

ABOUT

ROYAL POWERS

The world of Royal Powers is not so different from our own.
Except for the two mythical countries on the France/Spain border.
And the two extra royal families.
Oh, and that superpowers thing.
But otherwise, you know, pretty much the same.

CHAPTER ONE

When the trees opened out ahead of him, Alesander Fiala was tempted to turn his mare around and head back into the woods and the peace of his workshop. But a duke, even a disgraced one, couldn't hide forever. Eventually, his responsibilities—such as they were—would find him.

Sure enough, when he guided Berezi out onto the grassy hillside above the vineyards, the shadow of a falcon fell in front of her hooves. Sander scanned the clear blue sky. Hodei, his favorite peregrine, wasn't ridding the fields of nuisance birds today. For one thing, it was too early in the season. Fruit had set but hadn't ripened enough to interest marauding starling flocks yet. For another, Hodei was patrolling the edge of the woods, not the vineyard proper, and as soon as he spotted Sander on Berezi, he gave a cry and stooped, disappearing behind the ridge that hid Roses Manor from view.

A moment later, Sander's sister, Katalin, strode over the top, dressed in her usual no-nonsense hiking gear. Hodei gripped the leather gauntlet on her left arm, looking far too smug for a brown-feathered bird.

"Tattletale," Sander muttered, but he wasn't really annoyed. His sister was one of his favorite people in the world, one of the few who'd stood by him steadfastly through his troubles. Besides, it wasn't as if Hodei could avoid spilling everything to Katalin. Since her power was communicating with animals, Hodei wouldn't be able to resist telling her his news, especially since she'd probably brought him out expressly to find Sander.

Katalin gave a practiced toss and cast Hodei into the air again. She and Sander both took a moment to admire the peregrine's flight, but the view was marred by the sight of another figure—this one in green and yellow spandex—zooming across the sky.

Katalin grinned up at Sander. "If I didn't know you'd be out riding 24/7 at this time of year, my dear, dear brother, I'd have suspected you of dodging just to avoid Otho." She jerked her thumb at the retreating figure, his cape artistically spread in the air behind him.

"I don't avoid Otho," Sander returned mildly. "He visited me after the Disaster, just as you and Mother did."

"Only because you couldn't escape him then. You were his captive audience, with no choice but to listen to him drone on and on."

"Well, he is the royal messenger. Speaking is sort of his job."

"He's only the royal messenger because if Aunt Maialen sends him off with a message, it keeps him out from underfoot in the Castle and she can concentrate on running the country."

Sander swung down off Berezi so Katalin wouldn't have to crane her neck to talk to him. "Has she given him his power moniker yet? The last time he was here, he seemed certain it wouldn't be much longer."

Katalin sighed. "That was before the assassination attempt on Zorion. The Queen has more things to think about when her heir presumptive gets attacked than coming up with a name for such a minor power."

Sander winced. Their cousin had narrowly avoided serious injury, if not death, in that attack. It was only thanks to Zo's own powers that it hadn't been a disaster as great as... well... the Disaster. "I didn't know Zo could shape-shift into anything non-organic, let alone something as amorphous as a cloud."

"Aunt Maialen didn't either. That's one of the reasons she's so agitated."

"Still, I'd think she could take a few minutes to grant Otho his power moniker. He's been her courier for years now."

The two of them paced along the ridge above rows of vines showing the effects of the recent drought. "Except she doesn't really need a courier. Everyone has cell phones these days." She grimaced. "Sorry."

Sander smiled. "It's okay, Kat. You can say it. Everyone except me." He gave her a mock scowl. "I trust you left yours at the Manor before coming to find me."

She sighed. "I know the drill. I just wish it wasn't necessary."

"Believe me, nobody wishes that more than I do." He tucked her hand in his elbow. "You didn't have to come find me, you know. I was on my way back." He chuckled. "Luken made it very clear that if I don't finalize the details of my birthday dinner by six o'clock this evening, Chef Paul is going to serve nothing but beans on toast for the party."

"And nobody's scarier than your valet when he gets that *disappointed* look on his face." She squinted into the sun-bright sky, and if she was tracking Otho in flight, she was serious about avoiding a topic. "How do you suppose he gets his cape to fan like that? It doesn't even move in the wind."

Sander chuckled. "He had the royal tailors edge it with heavy gauge wire so it would hold its shape."

She stared at him, round-eyed. "You're joking."

"I swear I'm not. Luken told me, and he's never wrong. The next time you see Otho up close in his costume, check it out."

"Capes." She shook her head. "Didn't he learn *anything* from *The Incredibles*?"

Sander sighed. "I know he can be a bit pompous, but he's got a right to be a little sensitive about his power. If the only thing you can do is fly in a world with near instantaneous communication, you've got to be forgiven for feeling like obsolescence is creeping up on you." He patted her hand. "Come on now, Kat, out with it. You didn't come all this way on foot to discuss Otho's unfortunate costume choices."

"Weellll..." She grimaced, not meeting his gaze. "I'm leaving."

Alarm stiffened Sander's spine. "Leaving? But—"

"Not for long." She faced him and gripped his biceps. "I'll be back for your party, I promise."

His heart sank to his knees. "You won't be sailing with me." He didn't phrase it as a question. He could tell from the regret darkening the blue eyes so similar to his own.

"I'm sorry." She smiled shakily and pushed at an errant strand of dark hair that had escaped from her messy bun. "I've been dreaming of it for months. How could I help it? A whole week on the Mediterranean, relaxing on your boat."

"Gossiping with your seagull entourage?" Sander teased.

"I can't help it if they're chatty. But, Sander, I *know* the itinerary you set for us wouldn't have been your choice. It's *your* birthday cruise, and you picked every stop just for me."

He returned her smile, hoping it was convincing. "It's all right, Kat. I don't mind going alone."

"I know you don't, but you shouldn't have to. It's just..." Her shoulders rose with her sigh. "The Conservancy has a contract for me."

"A contract. You mean as Anime?"

She nodded. Their grandfather, the former King of South Abarra, had granted Katalin her power moniker when she was only seven and convinced then-Princess Maialen's newest Italian Greyhound puppy to stop peeing on the carpets in the throne room.

Katalin had always been precocious.

"They've rescued a young elephant from a poaching attempt in Tanzania. They're hoping I can calm her down and get a description of the perps."

"Oh, well," Sander said expansively, "if it's an *elephant*."

She punched him in the arm. "Shut up."

He grabbed her hand. "It's okay, Kat. I know you can never resist elephants. Just promise me one thing."

She eyed him warily. "What?"

"Promise me you won't set seagulls to spy on me and report back to you like every other time I've gone on a single-handed sail."

"I can't promise that. How else will I reassure Luken that you haven't fallen overboard?"

"You could trust that I know what I'm doing?"

"Trust has nothing to do with it. With no radio or electronics onboard, there's no other way we can contact you."

"You still can't. The gulls report to you, but they can't exactly talk to me. The only time I tried giving one a note, he ate it." Sander shaded his eyes, peering toward the southwest where Otho's yellow cape and green-clad legs were still visible. "I take it that's why Otho was here? To give you the message from the Conservancy?"

She scoffed. "Hardly. They emailed me the contract details as usual. No, Otho's message was for you."

"If he's wondering about his invitation to the party, I mailed it with the others last month. In fact, I've already gotten his RSVP." Otho was the only one, other than his mother and sister, who hadn't tendered regrets, the same as every other year since the Disaster.

"No. Aunt Maialen has a task for you."

Sander's jaw sagged. "Me? But she never has a task for me. Not since… Not since… well, you know when."

"Then all the more reason to take this one on, don't you think?" She jiggled his arm. "Prove to her that you're not a liability, Sander. Prove that you're smart and capable and *not dangerous*."

"But I am dangerous."

"You're not," she said hotly.

"Kat—"

"You haven't hurt anybody since the Disaster. That was seventeen years ago."

"I haven't hurt anybody because we've taken precautions. *Reasonable* precautions."

She pouted. "I don't call isolating yourself, retreating from the world out here, *reasonable*."

"I'm not retreating from the world." *Just keeping out of its way for its own good.* "This is my home. *Your* home, when you're not gallivanting all over the world at the Conservancy's beck and call. Mother's home, if she weren't kept too busy to leave her quarters at the Castle."

She bit her lip, staring out over the vines. "You could—"

"Stop, Kat. Please." He'd heard all the arguments before, repeated every year following that first dreadful one after the Disaster. Because whatever she was going to suggest, he *couldn't*.

He couldn't visit the Castle. He couldn't go into town. He couldn't fly in an airplane. He couldn't ride in most cars, for pity's sake. Not without endangering any electronic circuit within an undetermined range, not to mention every person *near* the electronic circuits, himself included.

"It's all right." He draped his arm across her shoulders, smiling down at her. "I'm not unhappy. Far from it. So." He gave her a squeeze and dropped his arm. "Why don't you tell me about this task the Queen has for me."

Katalin clenched her eyes shut and sucked in a breath. "She wants to you attend a meeting with the Duke of Arles about the drought in the northeastern fields." Her words tumbled over each other as if she were trying to keep him from interrupting again. She cracked an eyelid open and peeked up at him, probably to make sure he was still on his feet, because—

"The Duke of Arles?" His eyes nearly started out of his head. "She wants me to meet with *Wavelength*?"

"Actually, the Duke is demanding a meeting with Merrick Blackburn, but Aunt Maialen wants him to have backup and you're the only one who... who..."

Sander recovered enough to snort. "Who doesn't have anything better to do?"

"Well, think about it." She poked him in the chest, one of only three people on the planet who wasn't terrified to touch him. "It actually makes sense. Wavelength intercepts and transmits messages over the airwaves, and you don't ever send or receive any, because you don't have a cell phone or radio. Roses Manor is the only estate in all of South Abarra that doesn't have wi-fi."

"They want to meet at the Manor?" Sander's voice disappeared into a croak. Being in an enclosed space with other people? *No. Just no.* Roses Manor was as fortified against his rogue power as it was possible to be, but nobody was sure what his rogue power actually *was*.

Katalin shook her head, petting his arm as if she were soothing Berezi or one of the Manor greyhounds. "At Eagle's Oak, by the affected fields. It's not only our vines that are suffering. The North Abarran royal vineyards are right over the border."

"But—"

"And you're really the best person, anyway. You live next to the vineyard, so you know all about it."

"Yes, but I'm not *involved*." He couldn't enter the winery without endangering the equipment and the staff.

"What are you talking about? You're critical to Roses Estate wines."

He lifted an eyebrow. "I build barrels, Kat. By hand. Slowly. We could source them from a manufacturer quicker." He ran a hand through his hair. "Not cheaper, of course, since I don't charge anything, but—"

"Your barrels make a *difference*, Sander," she said, her tone fierce. "Ever since you started making them, Roses Estate vintages are *always* the highest rated Abarran wines, North or South. They *matter*." She moved in front of him and placed a gentle hand on his chest. "*You* matter."

He tucked that wayward strand of hair behind her ear. "I know I matter to you, dear heart, but let's be realistic. Everyone outside our family—and some inside it—still call me the Monster of Roses. I suspect Wavelength will be more likely to take my presence as an insult rather than respect my opinion."

Her expression turned stormy. "Then he's an idiot."

He chuckled, warmed by her loyalty. "While his temper is the stuff of legend, I've never heard anyone question his intelligence."

"You can be intelligent and still be an idiot," she muttered.

Sander took a deep breath. *Wavelength. Good lord. What a way to make my first official appearance as the Queen's representative.* Yet his aunt asked very little of him and had in fact been very kind to him over the years. He didn't hold it against her that she wouldn't allow Zorion to visit. Sander understood that, he really did. Zo was her only child, crown prince and heir presumptive. But Zo and Sander had been best friends as children. They actually shared the same birthday. Sander sent Zo an invitation to his birthday dinner every year, but Zo always returned sincere regrets, accompanied by a sumptuous present and one of his charmingly chatty letters.

"Surely Wavelength—*Arles*—isn't idiotic enough to blame this drought on Merrick."

Katalin dipped her chin and peered up at him from under her brows. "You're not isolated or innocent enough to believe *that*, are you?"

"But it's a widespread condition, not localized. Besides, Merrick can't make it rain when he's upset, and since that bloody tosser left him at the altar, he's barely managed an occasional sprinkle." However, the Queen had a point. If Sander was ill-equipped to go toe-to-toe with Wavelength, Merrick was probably worse, and he deserved to have someone at his back. The poor Duke of Camprodon was having a hard enough time lately without judgmental jerks like Arles getting on his case. Sander set his jaw. "All right. I'll do it. Has Arles's party been warned?"

"About no electronics? Yes. Auntie's message was clear on that point."

"Fine. When is the meeting?"

She bit her lip again. "Um, now?"

"Now?" Sander stumbled and had to catch himself with a hand on Berezi's withers. "What do you mean, now?"

"Well, in half an hour."

"Shit," Sander muttered. After a morning in his workshop, he'd spent all afternoon riding Berezi. Although he wasn't a complete sweaty mess, his riding clothes were definitely showing the signs of the warmth of the summer day. But half an hour? No way could he make it back to the Manor to change and still make the meeting, not without pushing the mare to her fastest pace. And he wouldn't do that. She was tired too after a couple of highly satisfying gallops by the lake.

He looked down at himself. "Which is the worst breach of protocol? Arriving in inappropriate clothing, or arriving late?"

"Late," Katalin said with no pause.

"Right." Merrick didn't deserve to face Wavelength's—the Duke of Arles's—notorious temper on his own. That would just stress him out more, and Sander had to admit that the Roses Estate vines needed rain as much as the Royal Crest fields across the border. "Berezi can carry us both for a ways, if you need to make your plane."

She waved him away. "No need. I left Ganix on the other side of the copse."

He tilted his head at her. "Why not ride him up here instead?"

She snorted. "Because I didn't want to hear his lovesick pining over Berezi, or his whining over her complete disdain, that's why." Berezi flicked one ear, and Katalin chuckled, patting her nose. "That's all right, love. Keep playing hard to get. It does him good to know he can't always get his way."

"Are you talking about Ganix or me?"

She dimpled at him. "I'll leave that for you to decide." She rose on her tiptoes in her sturdy boots and kissed his cheek. "Showing your face to others is definitely a good thing. Visibility, Sander. Embrace it. Now." She punched his arm again, but this time in encouragement. "Go show Duke Wavelength that he can't push us South Abarrans around."

Sander adjusted his collar. With so much still a mystery about his powers, could he really risk a meeting with so many unknowns? He'd spent the last seventeen years avoiding confrontation, just in case his own temper had contributed to the Disaster, although he didn't remember being angry at the time.

He sighed. The political relationship between North and South Abarra was always tense, even more so after the attempt on Zo's life, which South Abarran Intelligence was attributing to some kind of Northern plot. If something... *unfortunate* occurred to the Duke of Arles during the meeting, could it spark another armed skirmish? They still popped up like dandelions, even centuries after the Schism, when old Abarra had been split into North and South.

Sander just hoped he could maintain the same control he'd been practicing since he was fifteen, although he still wasn't entirely sure what he was supposed to be controlling. His life since then had been based entirely on *prevention*.

He just hoped this meeting with the Duke of Arles—with *Wavelength*—didn't require a whole boatload of political *cure*.

CHAPTER
TWO

"I can't *believe* this." Tarik Jaso slammed his desk drawer, startling his assistant into a flinch. "Sorry, Nico. I know this isn't your fault."

"Yes, Your Grace."

Tarik lifted an eyebrow. "You only call me *Your Grace* when you think I'm being an asshole."

Nico's olive skin flared with a blush. "I mean no disrespect."

"It's the *excess* of respect that's the problem. We came to terms with the informality I prefer by the end of your first week."

"Of course, Your— Tarik. But the instructions from the South Abarran envoy were quite specific. No—"

"Cameras, cell phones, or electronics of any kind allowed at the meeting. Trust me, I heard the blasted instructions." The way Tarik's powers worked, any message that concerned him, especially those directed here at his office in the vineyard with its special signal-enhancing equipment, was loud and clear even if he hadn't been listening for it— with special emphasis on the *loud*.

Fuck, my head is killing me.

He unloaded his cell phone from his inner jacket pocket, but before he could slam it on his desk, he recalled the dozen other broken phones that had suffered because he'd wanted to make a point. He set it down more gently—but still with intent.

"I suppose Queen Maialen is imposing this ludicrous restriction out of motherly jitters, given her heir was just targeted by some trigger-happy idiot in Dulibre?" Tarik buttoned his jacket. "The fool brought it on himself. He should have stayed in the southern part of the city where he belonged."

"I believe Crown Prince Zorion *was* in south Dulibre, but he was visiting a homeless shelter near the boundary."

"So nobody knows if the shot came from us or from them." Tarik *hmmmph*ed. "And now I'm paying the price." Okay, he was definitely being a jackass now. With his powers, he didn't *need* his cell phone to either send or receive messages. But it was the principle of the thing.

"Actually, the request—"

"You mean the demand?"

"The *request* is on behalf of the Duke of Roses." Nico's voice was carefully neutral, but Tarik gaped at him as if he'd shouted it from the rooftops.

"The Monster of Roses? What has he to do with anything?"

"He, ah, will be attending the meeting as the Queen's representative."

"Are you joking? The Queen is sending the fucking *Monster of Roses* to meet with me about a serious threat to North Abarran economy? That's... that's an *outrage*."

"Well, with the crown prince in seclusion, the Queen and Princess Enara deep in the investigation of the attack, and Prince Frantzisko out of the country, the Duke *is* the highest ranked South Abarran Royal who's available. Perhaps his participation should be viewed as an honor. An attempt to show that South Abarra is taking your concerns seriously."

"So seriously they're sending the most notorious murderer in their history to the meeting? Seems more like a slap in the face to me," Tarik muttered. "They only needed to send Camprodon anyway, since he's the one responsible."

Tarik glared out his office window at the browning leaves on his merlot vines. This field was the principal source of Royal Crest's premier Royal Velvet Blend and unless something happened tout de suite about the lack of rainfall, this year's vintage was going to be nonexistent—and he'd have even less of a chance of defeating Roses Estate at future Wine Internationale competitions. Not that he'd ever defeated them. But he had hopes. *As long as my fucking grapes don't turn into raisins before harvest.*

The roof of Roses Manor was visible atop its hill in the distance. When Tarik had taken over as operations director for the North Abarran royal vineyards, he'd insisted that the new facilities be built here, on the enemy's very doorstep, and made sure his vines extended right up to the border.

Keep your friends close and your enemies closer. Not that he had many friends. *Go figure.*

He'd expected to have a better chance of intercepting any messages from the Roses Estate winery or from Roses Manor itself here—which, if not strictly illegal according to those judgmental bastards in the Ministry of Powers, was certainly a gray area. *Stupid consent laws.* Except in the case of emergency or imminent loss of life, use of royal powers was forbidden without an explicit contract between the powered Royal—or supo, as the newscasters on both sides of the border referred to them in sneering voices—and the person requiring their services.

But as it happened, in all the years that he'd spent glaring at the Roses Estate fields beyond his own, he'd never intercepted a single message from that direction.

Highly suspicious. Maybe even criminal. Because why go to such lengths to conceal your communications unless you had something to hide?

Unless it's more sinister than that. In all the years since his power had manifested, nobody had ever discovered a way to selectively cut Wavelength's access to certain frequencies, although fuck knows they'd tried. *Hmmm. Could the Monster have found a way to bypass my power?* If that were the case, maybe this meeting wasn't the worst thing that could happen. *Better to know your enemies than get blindsided by them.*

He tugged his suit jacket straight and smoothed his lapels. "All right. Let's go."

As he strode out of his office onto the deck that overlooked the fields with Nico at his heels, he picked up his cousin's voice on the exclusive royal frequency.

"Tarik."

"Your Majesty."

Bastien's chuckle rippled through the airwaves. *"It's remarkable how clearly your sarcasm registers even when you aren't actually speaking. You're missing the party. Again."*

Tarik charged down the steps. *"Considering it's one of many, I'll survive."*

"Tarik. I give these courtship parties entirely for your benefit. It's a little difficult for you to find a consort if you don't actually attend them."

"That hardly matters. You want me to make a strategic match. Fine. I'm game. Just pick the one who'll work best for your political agenda. You know I don't care."

Bastien sighed. *"You have the capacity to care. You're demisexual, not sociopathic."*

"So once I get to know them, we'll build a relationship and I'll be fine."

"The problem with that scenario is that you never bother to get to know anyone. That's the purpose of these parties. For you to find somebody you want *to know—and who won't be completely repulsed when they get to know* you, *which might be the more difficult task."*

"Nice, Bas. I love you too. And speaking of repulsed, did you know Queen Maialen is sending the Monster of Roses to this meeting?"

There was a pause, Bastien obviously as surprised as Tarik had been. *"No. I hadn't heard that."*

"Well, it's true. And apparently His Monstrous Grace has decreed there are to be no cell phones, cameras, or electronics of any kind. How's Nico supposed to take notes at the meeting? With a fucking goose feather quill?"

This time Bastien laughed outright. *"You've been singing your so-exemplary assistant's praises since his first day on the job. Surely he's capable of transcribing your deathless proclamations with a humble pen and paper."*

"That's beside the point. What's the Monster afraid of? What's he hiding?"

While Bastien paused, Tarik strode uphill between two rows of vines, Eagle's Oak, the designated meeting place, in sight.

"Have you ever thought, mon cousin, *that 'Monster' may be a very cruel way for people to refer to a physical disfigurement? He was at the epicenter of the most significant South Abarran tragedy in the last century."*

Tarik slowed his steps. *Fuck.* He'd never thought of that. Now he felt like an asshole. Well, more of an asshole than usual. *"Has anyone seen him since then?"*

"Not outside his family."

"In seventeen years? That seems... unlikely."

"Nevertheless, it's the truth. Now. Have you taken your ibuprofen?"

Tarik speeded up again. *"That only masks the pain."*

"That's the idea, you idiot. You don't have to diagnose the headaches—you know what causes them. Take the painkillers, at least until you can soak in one of those decadent bathtubs of yours."

Tarik chuckled this time, earning a quizzical glance from Nico, who of course couldn't hear his exchange with Bastien. *"You're just envious because you don't have anything like them at the New Palace."*

"I don't have time to loll about in a bath. As it is, I have to almost shut down the government to grab a quick shower. Now go to your meeting and try not to punch anybody."

Tarik scowled at the rows of wilting vines that marched up the hill ahead of him. *"I don't punch people."*

"Maybe not with your fists," Bastien drawled. *"We'll talk later."*

Tarik glanced at Nico. He didn't look disturbed by Tarik reacting to apparently nothing during the silent communication with Bastien. But then, he'd been Tarik's assistant for nearly two months—far longer than any of his predecessors had lasted. He was used to it by now.

Tarik glanced up at towering Eagle's Oak, the sole tree on the hill's crest, left in place because its massive trunk spanned the border and neither North nor South Abarra could ever agree whom it belonged to, and therefore who was responsible for removing it. One way or another, he'd get satisfaction today. He was more than happy to leave the political nonsense to Bastien, but when it came to economics, even the king bowed to Tarik's authority. South Abarra would learn they couldn't threaten North Abarra without consequences.

"Ready?" he asked Nico, who nodded, brandishing his— *God*—ballpoint pen. Tarik strode the last few meters and topped the hill to stand in the oak's shade. The border between the two vineyards—between the two countries— was marked with nothing sturdier than a split rail fence. Well, two fences, with a neutral gap of about three meters between them where the actual border ran, the oak smack on top of it.

Tarik stopped, frowning. Nobody was there. "What time is it?"

Nico didn't hesitate. "Five oh one."

A minute past the stated meeting time, exactly as Tarik had planned, calculated precisely to show *he* had nothing to atone for. Punctuality was a matter of respect, but early arrival was for the guilty party. If the Southerners weren't here to witness his perfect timing, however, it lost all its impact—and pissed him off because if *they* were late, it meant they weren't granting this issue its proper urgency.

He scanned the field on the south side of the fence. He could make out two people cowering next to a wheelbarrow far enough away that shouting at them would be undignified. He couldn't march down and confront them either. He couldn't set foot on southern lands without permission or a fucking diplomatic visa.

He opened himself up, scanning the airwaves for messages that might explain why the Monster and his crew hadn't bothered to keep their commitments, but as usual, there were no emissions from the Roses lands. But—

"... meet... job... monster... bomb..."

Tarik snapped his head around. Where had that come from? Somewhere... west? But was it from the north or the south? Was it a serious threat or just somebody complaining about a terrible movie or ordering an unfortunate drink? If he could just concentrate past the pounding in his temples...

But then he realized that the pounding wasn't only in his head. *Hoofbeats.* Good lord, somebody was actually trotting up the hill on a *horse*. Tarik had to give him points for style, but this wasn't the Middle Ages, for fuck's sake. The man pulled his mount up next to the men lurking behind the wheelbarrow, and then the three of them continued up the hill toward him, stopping just shy of the fence.

"Good afternoon. Or, I suppose it's nearly evening, isn't it?" The rider peered at the sky. "I hadn't realized… Oh. I'm sorry." He dismounted and inclined his head, an acknowledgement between equals. "Alesander Fiala, Duke of Roses."

For a moment Tarik could only stare. *This* was the Monster of Roses? This sturdy, broad-chested man with the sun-streaked brown hair and eyes the color of the Mediterranean? *No visible disfigurement there.* Nothing but an undeniably beautiful man in brown knee-high boots and buff-colored pants—*incredibly tight* buff-colored pants—that unexpectedly made Tarik's mouth water. *WTF?*

The Monster caught Tarik's stare and his cheeks colored, which rendered him even more attractive. *Fuck. What is wrong with me?*

"I apologize for my attire. I was only informed of the meeting half an hour ago while I was out on a ride and didn't have time to change or I'd risk being late." He glanced around. "Although since I'm the last one here, I suppose I'm late after all."

One of the men behind the Monster cleared his throat. The Monster startled, flushing deeper. "Oh, ah, may I present His Grace the Duke of Camprodon—" He gestured to the third man, a slender blond who was shifting uneasily from foot to foot. Tarik eyed Camprodon critically. He supposed the man was technically more classically gorgeous than the Monster, but he looked as if the slightest wind would carry him away. "And this is Joseba Luken, my —"

"Enough," Tarik barked and pointed. "You. Camprodon. Why the fuck are you destroying my grapes?"

Camprodon startled like a frightened hare. "I— I'm sorry?"

"You should be. What is this, some kind of plot to compromise the North Abarran economy? Disrupt our supply chain? Are you pissed because we ship out nearly twice as much product as you southerners do?"

Camprodon shared a panicked glance with the Monster. "I don't know what you—"

"Come off it." Tarik was being an asshole. He *knew* it. But with the adorably flustered Monster staring at him as if he had two heads, it was as though that rogue supo, Mastermind, had taken over his brain. *Because I don't ever think anyone is adorable.* Adorable *isn't in my vocabulary.* Besides, this was obviously Camprodon's doing. "Everyone knows what you do, *Rainmaker*," Tarik sneered. "So why'd you stop making rain over my fields? I'll wager the Camprodon vineyards—what do you call them?" *As if I don't know perfectly well, but all in aid of negotiations.* "Hearts and Hands?"

"Hand to Heart," Camprodon said faintly.

"Just so," Tarik scoffed. "I'll wager the Hand to Heart crop is doing just fine."

"As a matter of fact," Camprodon began, "our vines are —"

"Don't bother denying it. Look at the evidence." Tarik swept his hand wide, indicating his withering vines. "Right there."

Camprodon took a step back. "I—"

"Now just a bloody minute." The Monster put a hand on Camprodon's back, and for some reason, that ratcheted Tarik's temper up another notch. "You're not the only one suffering. This whole region is experiencing a drought. Hand to Heart is affected too, as is Roses Estate. And if you want evidence…" He mirrored Tarik's arm sweep, an obvious mockery. "Take a look at our fields."

Tarik snorted. "I'm sure you can afford the appearance of hardship if it supports your conspiracy to attack our country."

"*Our* conspiracy?" The Monster's eyes narrowed. "It was *our* crown prince who was shot at just this week. *That* was an attack. This—" There was that mocking arm sweep again, a gesture Tarik grudgingly admired. *Couldn't have done it better myself.* "This is *nature*. This is global warming. This is the risk we take as viniculturists."

"Act of God, is it?" Tarik's tone dripped scorn. Was it too over the top? *Nah.* Anyway, he was almost vibrating to see how the Monster would counter. *Come on, guy, show me what you've got.* "I'd buy that more if you weren't standing next to a supo who can literally make rain fall from a cloudless sky."

Camprodon raised a shaking finger. "Actually, um, I need at least a small cloud."

"Right. You probably steal them from others' skies to suit yourself."

"Leave him alone." The Monster lurched forward, reaching the fence. "His powers don't work that way, and even if they did, he'd never do anything that cruel."

Nice. Loyalty and protectiveness. Too bad it's misplaced. "That you know of," Tarik drawled.

The Monster's fists clenched at his sides. "I wouldn't expect *you* to understand. *You* know nothing of kindness or compassion or… or…" His eyes widened suddenly and one hand crept to his chest. He staggered back. "No. Not again. I can't…" He spun, and with his mare following him like a puppy, he grabbed the other two men by their elbows and towed them down the hill where he muttered something to them and jumped on his horse.

And fucking *galloped away.*

"I don't fucking *believe* it." Tarik lunged for the fence, but Nico stepped in front of him.

"I'm sorry, Your Grace, but you can't. You haven't been granted permission to cross onto their lands."

"But— But he can't just ride off in the middle of negotiations."

Nico pressed his lips together. "It's possible he thought he was riding off to avoid an international incident. If I may say so, you did come in a bit hot, Your Grace."

If Nico was *Your Gracing* him again, Tarik figured he really had overstepped. And when he thought back on his behavior? *Fuck. I'm an asshole.*

"You're right." His gaze snagged on his poor wilting vines. His grapes. His legacy. His *passion*. Bastien had warned him not to punch anybody, and he'd stepped right up and done that very thing, even if it wasn't with his fists. "I'll tender my apologies." He jabbed a finger in Nico's direction. "But that doesn't mean this is over. Camprodon still needs to answer for this. I'm sure he could make it rain if he wanted to. He just doesn't want to give me the satisfaction."

He started down the hill toward his office, Nico keeping pace but always a step behind.

"… *bomb… soon… riot… kill…*"

Tarik's steps faltered. The fragmented message didn't have a discernable voice, which meant it wasn't part of a cell phone conversation. Internet chat? Shortwave radio narrowcast? But the repeated word—*bomb*—made him believe it was related to that first one. And coming so close to his meeting with the Monster, who was also mentioned in the first fragment? They had to be related.

Related and a threat.

He needed to get back to his office where he could scan for more. He glanced sidelong at Nico. If Tarik was about to dive into the gray area of listening in on conversations he'd not been contracted for, he needed to keep Nico out of it. The authorities often looked the other way when a high-ranking Royal broke the rules. They were less forgiving to any commoner under suspicion.

Nico following without question, Tarik took the long way to the office across the now-empty loading dock, detouring through the vast tank room, where the last of the crew were just finishing up. *Good. Nobody in the building except the two of us.*

He sat down at his desk and rifled in its drawers until he found a pen. Fuck, Bastien would bust a gut if Tarik ever told him he'd stooped to writing a note. In fact... He smirked and dashed off a note to Bastien too, informing him of the messages. *There.* Technically, he'd now reported the incident, but since Bastien wouldn't get the notice until later tonight or tomorrow, Tarik would have time to conduct his less-than-sanctioned investigation.

He folded both notes and stuck them into Royal Crest envelopes. "I'm sorry to do this, Nico, but I've got two errands for you at the New Palace. Notify Jacques to pick you up right away. He can take you by your flat to pick up anything you might need."

"Of course." Nico smiled politely as he sent the text to Tarik's driver. "And you needn't apologize for asking me to do my job."

"Yes. Well." Tarik cleared his throat. "I need you to pick up my new suit for the Northern Hope Medal ceremony." In truth, Bastien had been bugging him to get the damn thing for weeks, but Tarik had figured he'd just avoid the hassle and change at the Palace before the ceremony. "The royal tailors have it. By the time you get there, they'll be gone for the day, so stay over in my quarters." He handed the first note to Nico. "This'll ensure they release it to you."

Nico took the envelope. "You shock me, Tarik.

Uh-oh. Did Nico realize Tarik was trying to pull a fast one? "How so?"

"You've stooped to writing instead of just sending a message to the receiver at the palace."

Tarik chuckled with relief. "The royal tailors are traditionalists. They'll be less likely to look down their noses at you if you use communication methods that are as old as they are." He handed over the second note. "This one is for the King. I'd prefer you deliver it personally, so don't worry about hurrying back if you have to wait for an audience."

Nico tucked both notes inside his portfolio, glancing uncertainly from Tarik to the door. *Ah*. He'd made it a point of honor to never leave the building before Tarik did, so Tarik rose and strolled out of the office.

Nico pulled the door closed behind him. "Do you need Jacques to drop you at your villa on the way?"

"No, no. I plan to stroll through the fields for a while." Tarik's jaw tightened. "Assess the damage. I'll see you tomorrow."

"All right."

Tarik stood, hands in his pockets, until Jacques pulled up in the Royal Crest Bentley and Nico climbed into the rear seat. To keep up appearances, in case Nico was looking out the window, Tarik strolled into the fields, opposite the way they'd walked for the meeting. But as soon as the car turned out of the massive stone gates and disappeared around a bend, he raced back to the winery.

He walked all the way around it, making sure no cars remained next to the loading dock and that all the workers had departed. Satisfied, he strode onto the deck outside his office. But as he was keying his code into the security pad, he heard a creak behind him. Before he could turn, pain bloomed at the back of his skull.

As he dropped to his knees, he felt the prick of a needle in his neck and a voice rasped, "Bon voyage, Your Grace."

CHAPTER THREE

Sander spent an extra hour rubbing Berezi down when he got back from the abortive meeting. God, what the Duke of Arles must think of him. He frowned as he teased a knot out of Berezi's silky mane. *He doesn't want to know what I think of him.*

"Bloody asshole," he muttered, and then winced. *Sounds like an unfortunate medical condition.* Berezi flicked an ear, clearly agreeing with him. He patted her neck and handed the currycomb to a disapproving groom. "Thanks for reserving judgment, sweet girl."

He nodded to the groom and strode out of Berezi's stall into the stable proper, the heels of his boots clicking when he stepped from the earthen floor of the stall to the wooden planks lining the hallway. Every stride seemed to echo his failure.

I shouldn't have run. I should have stood my ground and advocated properly for Merrick. The poor Duke had clearly been blindsided by Arles as much as Sander had been. *If I'd kept a cooler head. If I'd countered with logic instead of emotion. If I'd brought more "fight" and not so much "flight."*

But something about Arles's springy dark curls, his nearly black eyes, his warm brown skin, so dissonant with the vitriol spewing out of his full lips, had caused a... a *pressure* inside Sander to build and build and *build*, until he was certain it was about to burst free. And the last time that had happened, it had been a disaster.

Correction: It had been *the* Disaster.

So he'd fled and used his lovely, patient Berezi to calm himself down.

He made his way into his wing of the Manor where he found Luken waiting for him, as Sander had known he would be. Sander smiled wryly. "Made a right shambles of that, didn't I?" He huffed a soft laugh. "I suspect this will be the last time the Queen asks for my help with a task."

"On the contrary, Your Grace. I believe walking away from the table—well, from the fence, in this case—was the correct move. Clearly His Grace of Arles was in no mood to listen."

Sander glanced curiously at Luken as they ascended the curved oak staircase to Sander's quarters. "Have you met him before?"

"I have never had the pleasure." Luken's tone was as dry as library dust.

"I don't think you've had the pleasure yet. None of us have. Because a more unpleasant fellow I've never met." Not that he'd met many people since the Disaster. Sander sighed. "Still, I should have controlled my temper better, for Merrick's sake."

"Temper, Your Grace?"

"Yes." Sander paused at the top of the stairs, one hand on the newel post's finial, carved in the shape of a half-open rose. "I can't take credit for timing my exit for Merrick's benefit, or as a statement on Arles's less-than-optimal company manners. I... I *felt* something, Luken. In here." Sander tapped his chest with a closed fist.

Luken's eyebrows rose a fraction, the equivalent of *Holy shit!* from his imperturbable valet. "You mean something related to your powers?"

Sander nodded. "I couldn't stay. Not and risk you or Merrick, or God forbid, create an international incident by injuring King Bastien's favorite cousin. So I ran. Well, Berezi ran, and kindly allowed me to accompany her."

"Perhaps..." Luken's tone was measured, careful. "Perhaps you should forgo your birthday sail, Your Grace. Since Her Highness is not able to accompany you."

"No!" Just the thought of losing the peace of floating under the stars, far away from the incessant hum of civilization, was enough to rekindle that *build*. "That's the last thing I should do. Sailing—especially sailing alone—centers me, Luken. You know that."

"Yes, but under the circumstances—"

"Under the circumstances, I can't afford *not* to go." He smiled and gripped Luken's shoulder. "Trust me, my friend. I've had seventeen years to figure out *that* much."

"Very well. Shall I draw your bath?"

"Yes, thank you. And afterward, I'll dash off a note to the Duke of Arles, requesting another meeting at a time of his choosing." Sander entered his bedroom and sat on the stool by the door so Luken could help him remove his boots. "Although this time, I'll come armed with a little more data about the effects of the drought on South Abarran vineyards."

After he'd bathed and changed into lounge pants and a dressing gown, Sander ate a light meal in his room so as not to inconvenience the staff since he was the only Royal in residence. Then he sat down at his desk to at least attempt to behave like a responsible adult—one who was technically a prince as well as a duke.

Thank goodness his unfortunate condition didn't affect his use of his grandfather's fountain pen. With it snug in his hand, he was able to find the words, scribing them on his personal stationery in the copperplate script he'd had nearly two decades to perfect.

After his note to Arles, he kept going, writing to his vineyard manager and to the Queen's Minister of Agriculture, requesting any information he could reasonably share to counter Arles's accusations. He penned a note of apology to Merrick, assuring him of future support. As he sealed the envelope with his ducal crest, he added a silent hope that the gentle man would be able to conquer the grief and humiliation that had overwhelmed him after his cretin of a fiancé had married someone else for money. *Especially considering said cretin is my own second cousin.*

With a feeling of accomplishment, he retired to bed. But after hours of tossing and turning, with Arles's words swirling in his mind, Arles's dark eyes—fiercer than any falcon's—boring into his, Arles's curly shoulder-length hair dancing gaily in the breeze in complete opposition to his attitude, Sander gave up.

Since Katalin wasn't coming along on this sail, there was no need for him to delay until tomorrow, when they'd planned to cast off. He tossed the bedclothes aside and stalked to the desk, using the pen to write a last note, this one to Luken.

I've decided to leave for my sail early and take an extra day. Don't worry—I'll be back in a week, in time for my birthday dinner. And you may rest assured that Katalin won't be able to resist encouraging those dreadful gossipy seagulls to keep an eye on me.

Thank you, my friend. I am ever grateful for your support.

In the dim light, he dressed in his UV tech shorts and T-shirt and slipped on his deck shoes. He hesitated with his windbreaker in his hand. *Wear it or pack it?* He eyed his rucksack and duffel on the closet floor. *Wear it. Definitely.* Heaven forbid that he disarrange the pristine packing job. With Luken's usual unobtrusive efficiency, he'd readied the bags a week ago, just as he'd arranged with the marina staff to prep *Askatasun* for a cruise with Katalin on board.

Sander chuckled as he made his way through the darkened manor. Katalin never sailed without twice the number of towels and linens than Sander felt were necessary, but it wouldn't exactly inconvenience him to have the extras onboard. The provisions were bound to be ready to load too. He could use the handcart to transport them to the boat himself without needing to rouse any of the staff.

Yes, this was the right decision. He was certain of it. A week at sea, a week to feel normal, to feel ordinary, to feel like less of a burden to his family, was exactly what he needed.

As he walked through the formal gardens and down the path to the marina, he gave thanks again to the ancestor—a long-ago duchess—who'd insisted that her home be within sight of the sea. Sander had reaped the benefit all his life, and never stepped onto the dock, his own *Askatasun* bobbing in the water next to the *Enara*, his father's larger yacht, without acknowledging that debt.

His throat tightened at the sight of *Enara*, named for his mother. He kept hoping she'd take it out. But she never had. Not since his father's death. The marina staff kept it in excellent repair, ready to sail at a moment's notice. *I should really ask them to put it in dry dock. It's not doing anybody any good in the water.*

He dropped his duffel and rucksack next to the marina's big metal door, punched his code into the security keypad, and rolled the door open in a *swoosh* of well-oiled bearings.

After every sail, the marina crew stripped *Askatasun* of all remaining supplies other than basic spices and donated them to food banks in Dulibre, so the hand-truck was fully loaded with cases of water and non-perishable food, as well as net bags of oranges, grapes, and mangoes—Katalin's favorite. *Askatasun* had no refrigeration facilities, just as it had no electronics or radio equipment or anything mechanical that might react poorly to Sander's... condition. He'd made sure of it when he'd built the boat with his own hands. But the fruit would stay fresh for a week, especially if he ate the grapes first.

Sander grabbed the cart's handle and pushed it out onto the dock just as dawn was turning the sky a luminous gray. He wheeled past his luggage and down the half dozen meters to where *Askatasun* was moored. But his steps slowed when he spotted the bow line dangling against the hull, no longer tied off on the dock cleat. The marina crew—and Sander himself—would *never* allow that to happen. And was that... was that...

The sound of splintering wood rose from below *Askatasun*'s deck. Sander's heart bumped sideways and heat rose behind his eyes. *Someone's on my boat. Someone's hurting my boat.*

"Who's there? What the hell are you doing?" He dropped the cart handle and raced the last few feet to jump onto the lazarette, the storage locker aft of the helm, *Askatasun* dipping under his weight.

The intruder uttered a muffled curse. Then someone wearing a black balaclava loomed in the companionway. He stepped out into the cockpit. *God, he's big.* He was followed by another person, smaller, also masked and—

"Hey! That's my ax. Give it back."

The larger guy laughed and Sander realized it was monumentally stupid to face down two men, one of whom was twice his size and the other who was holding a very serviceable murder weapon. The boat wasn't that big—not quite sixteen meters from bow to stern, her beam just over three—so there wasn't much maneuvering room to dodge possibly homicidal intruders.

But this boat was *his*, damn it. *Askatasun* was *his*.

Something started to build again, and he clenched his fists, jaw working. *Come on, stupid out-of-control power. Be useful for once.* He braced himself for the guys to rush him, hoping his tae kwon do lessons were good for something besides physical fitness. But they didn't approach him. Instead they scrambled onto the dock, and the one with the ax chopped *Askatasun*'s stern line, setting her adrift.

Then he met Sander's gaze through his mask, grinned maliciously, and dropped the ax into the water. They took off at a run, leaving nothing but the echoes of their laughter.

"Bastards! When I—"

Askatasun lurched, heeling sharply to starboard, so Sander half-fell into the cockpit, grabbing onto the helm to keep from toppling overboard.

How is this happening? The sea was preternaturally calm this morning.

Another lurch, and the boat righted itself, but as Sander's jaw sagged, *Askatasun* rose into the air, accompanied by the sound of the sea being sucked from the rocks below the quay.

"What the—" Sander crept to the edge of the cockpit, one hand still clutching the wheel in case the boat should heel again, and peered over the gunwale.

His jaw dropped further until it was possibly at his knees, because *Askatasun* was borne up by a column of water, her rudder catching nothing but air. Sander tried to see more, but a dense fog suddenly engulfed him, obscuring his vision of anything more than a hand-span in front of his face.

"Whoa!" Sander clutched the wheel, because suddenly *Askatasun* was hauling ass, clearly faster than her normal top speed of sixteen knots, the wind of her passage making Sander's eyes tear up.

If she heels again at this rate, I'll get launched overboard for certain. Keeping his hold on the helm, he lowered himself to the deck. Pieces of rope littered the cockpit. *Damn that ax man. What else did he do to my poor* Askatasun? Sander stretched his arm, fingers extended to their fullest, back muscles protesting, and scrabbled one of the scraps to his chest before it was tossed into the air by the wind. He threaded it through his belt and lashed himself to a deck cleat.

Then he lay face down and held on for all he was worth.

The roar of the wind didn't mask *Askatasun*'s creaks and groans. *God, please don't let the mast snap.* Thank goodness the sails were still furled or they would have been ripped away. Could he reach a life vest in the lazarette? *What good will a life vest do me when I'm rocketing through the air?*

He swallowed, hard. At some point, this had to end, but how? With *Askatasun* smashed against the cliffs of Montecristo, Sander crushed in the wreckage? With poor *Askatasun* finally surrendering to the stress of a speed she wasn't intended for and dumping Sander into the Mediterranean, ten meters or more below? A life vest *might* come in handy then, if the fall didn't kill him first.

He raised his head, his eyes watering in the wind, but couldn't see anything through the fog. Since fog and wind didn't naturally hang out together, Sander had to conclude that it was part of the current unnatural transportation method. But what was its purpose? To prevent Sander from seeing his location?

Or to prevent others from seeing the phenomenon?

Because this had to be the work of a supo. Localized tidal waves with attendant fog banks just didn't occur in nature.

But who? And why? It's not as if Sander were that important to anyone except his family. He was the Monster of Roses, for pity's sake. Nobody would touch him—either politically or socially—with a barge pole. And full riot gear.

His nose began to run, as it always did in the wind. He scrabbled his handkerchief out of the pocket of his shorts so he could wipe it. He sniffed. *Why can't I smell the sea?* Oddly enough, all he could detect over the familiar scents of *Askatasun* herself was a faint whiff of wine.

The ax. The sound of splintering wood. Damn it. The vandals must have destroyed at least one of the kegs of Roses Estate wine he kept on board. *They better not have broken both of them.*

He rested his forehead against the deck, laughing weakly although his breath was nearly stolen by the wind. He was hurtling toward God only knew what fate and the only thing that worried him was the loss of his onboard wine stash? If that was the only casualty when this was over, he'd count himself lucky.

He stroked *Askatasun*'s deck. "You'll carry me home safely, old girl. You always have. You always will."

Askatasun lurched, as if responding to his murmur, and Sander raised his head. Was the wind not quite as strong? Were they slowing? Yes, they were definitely slowing. How long had this been going on? How far had they come? Where was—

With a sickening *crunch*, *Askatasun* stopped dead, flinging Sander against the helm and knocking him breathless. He inched over onto his back, his ribs crying out in protest, and lay there, attempting to draw in air, as the fog dissipated to reveal a cloudless sky, the sun only halfway to its zenith.

Since Sander had hit the dock before six... Good lord, he'd been traveling for *three hours*. It hadn't seemed like that... Wait. It had been six at home, on the coast of South Abarra, in the same time zone as Barcelona. *If I traveled east, then—* He laughed weakly. *Of course I traveled east.* Since South Abarra was at the far western shore of the Mediterranean, there wasn't anywhere else he could go. *Unless the supernatural tidal wave could travel over land.*

At this point, Sander couldn't discount the possibility.

With shaking fingers, he untied himself from the cleat and pushed himself to his feet. He staggered across the cockpit and peeked over the gunwale. *Holy...* He clenched his eyes shut, his knees nearly buckling, because he'd found the source of that sickening crunch.

An enormous boulder, probably a third of *Askatasun's* length overall, was embedded in her starboard hull amidship.

He took a breath and opened his eyes, squinting against the glare. Where had he put his sunglasses? *Oh right.* They were back on the dock, along with his luggage and all the provisions for the trip. So no food. Very little, if any, water, because even if the starboard water tank had survived the impact—which he doubted—it wouldn't have been full, anyway. Sander had intended to fill both tanks himself before setting sail, since the crew wouldn't have had it on their schedule until later today.

Sander sank down on the lazarette. So now here he was. Shipwrecked. His poor *Askatasun* breached and beached. He peered over the transom. Was that... Yes, it was. Her rudder was lying at the water's edge ten meters away, bobbing in the gentle waves.

"God *damn* it!" Sander slammed his fists into his thighs. But swearing wouldn't repair his boat. He wasn't overly concerned with survival. If he couldn't find help wherever this was, he had an emergency kit with water pouches and unappetizing but nutritious rations. If he was careful, he could last until Katalin finished soothing the traumatized elephant and was back in communication with her seagull snitches. A week at most. No problem. Boredom would probably be more of an issue than hunger and thirst.

He limped for the companionway, the scent of spilled wine growing stronger. When he peered down into the cabin, he saw the glint of sun on liquid, but the liquid wasn't dark enough to be undiluted wine. *Yep, the starboard water tank is toast.* Oh well. If he was lucky, the port tank might have enough in it to afford at least one shower before rescue arrived.

He sighed and descended into the cabin, trying not to look at the rock face where the spare bunk—Katalin's bunk —used to be. He huffed in disgust at the splintered wine keg floating in its ex-contents. At least they hadn't found the other keg, the vintage that he and Katalin planned to taste on the cruise.

I can lounge on deck, getting soused and singing pirate songs while waiting for the gulls to find me. He'd certainly spent time in worse ways over the past seventeen years.

The mattress from the destroyed bunk had gotten flung off, although it was somehow propped clear of the diluted wine. *Good. One less thing to clean up.* Sander lifted it, ready to haul it above deck, but what lay under it made it slip from his suddenly numb fingers.

Because there, sprawled face up with his curls fanned out and lifting in the ripples raised by Sander's steps, lay the Duke of Arles.

Shit.

CHAPTER FOUR

Tarik's head was *killing* him. He moaned. This wasn't the normal headache he got from using his powers—that always stabbed right through his temples like a blindfold of pain. This was different. The base of his skull throbbed, and it felt like his brain was trying to hack its way out to escape the agony. *Bastien was right. I should have taken the fucking ibuprofen.*

But he had a feeling ibuprofen wouldn't fix this. His mouth was dry, his tongue like a block of sandpaper. His eyelids were stuck together, eyelashes gritty, but that was fine. That was okay. He didn't want to open them anyway, because he was fairly certain any light would slice his head right in half. Just split it like a fucking melon.

He was vaguely aware that he was wet. Well, part of him: his back, from his head to his heels, and since he was still wearing a suit, moisture wicking into the fabric, he obviously wasn't floating in one of his tubs or the infinity pool. *If I were floating, I wouldn't be lying on something this fucking hard.*

Wait. There. To my right. The soft sound of wood against wood, like someone closing a cabinet door. *Where am I?* He uncurled his fist and patted the floor next to his body. His fingers splashed in some kind of liquid and by the smell, at least some of it had to be wine.

"Oh, thank goodness. You're awake." The voice was vaguely familiar, but Tarik heard so many voices that he couldn't place it. Not with his head pounding like the North Abarran Drum Corps had taken up residence. With another soft thump, Tarik felt the heat of another person next to his hip and suddenly he started to shiver.

"I'm not sure this counts as awake," he croaked.

His unknown companion responded with a sound low in his throat, a sound of concern. "How do you feel?"

"Like somebody used my head as a hammer to carve that stupid stone monument on Mount Abarra." *I should really open my eyes.* But it seemed like so much fucking *work.* Maybe if he drifted off again, the headache would be better when he awoke again.

"Hey." The guy patted Tarik's cheek with a callused palm.

Must be one of the workers from the winery. Right. *I was at the winery. That's why there's wine.* "But I don't bathe in wine. That would be a waste."

"I'm sure it would. But I don't think you should go back to sleep."

Another pat, and Tarik wasn't sure if he wanted to bat the guy's hand away or hold it to his cheek, because there was something in that touch...

He cracked his eyes open. "Holy fuck!" He scrambled to sit up, to back away, only to get hit by a wave of nausea and dizziness. He fought it, fought *hard*, because right there? Looming over him like the promise of retribution?

The fucking Monster of Roses.

The Monster held out a hand as if to touch Tarik again. *Not happening.* Tarik scooted back on his ass only to smash his head against something. "Ow! Fucking hell." He peered up at what seemed to be a wall of rock in what was otherwise a rather posh wood-paneled room. Small oval windows near its unreasonably low ceiling splashed sunlight over the Monster's face, catching on the sun-blond streaks in his brown hair.

As Tarik's brain came further back online, he realized where he was. Hell, he'd been on enough yachts in his time to recognize the inside of a boat when he saw it. But this boat wasn't going anywhere with a giant boulder jammed through its hull.

A scrap of memory drifted back to him. *The vineyard. My office. Getting coshed on the head.* Then the prick of a needle and the voice, *"Bon voyage, Your Grace,"* as if they'd known he'd end up on a boat.

And before that, the messages, the threat, the *plot.* Just as he'd suspected, the Monster was at the center of it. He tried to push through the pain and transmit a message to Nico, to Bastien, to *somebody.* If he could just pick up another person's frequency, no matter how banal their conversation, he could hijack the signal and order them to contact the authorities.

But there was nothing. No chatter on any frequency. No constant barrage of colliding transmissions in the airwaves. Panic battered at his ribcage. He might as well be parked in one of his bathtubs, with water surrounding him and granting him blessed peace from the cacophony.

Have I complained about the cacophony? I'll never complain again, as long as somebody hears me now and rescues me from the Monster.

The Monster crouched in front of him, a pretty fair approximation of concern on his face. "I'm afraid you might have a concussion."

"You think?" Tarik spat. "That's what happens when you hit someone on the head hard enough to knock them out."

The Monster's eyes widened. "I didn't hit you." He held out a small packet of some kind, like a single-dose painkiller from a first aid kit, as well as a pouch of water.

Tarik glared at the pills and water. *If I can hold on to the anger, I can banish the terror.* But with the way his heart was trying to leap out of his chest, success wasn't exactly guaranteed. "I suppose you didn't drug me either. I suppose you're not trying to drug me now."

"What?" He blinked, then his blue eyes turned stormy. "I didn't hit you and I didn't drug you."

"No? Then where are we?" The Monster bit his lip. *Aha! Got you!* Tarik slapped the deck. "What is this?"

"It's my boat. *Askatasun.*"

"So I wake up on *your* boat, after having been bashed and drugged, but you had nothing to do with it?"

"I most certainly did not." He pointed at the rock protruding through the boat's hull. "If you haven't noticed, I'm in the same situation you are. I'd hardly have wrecked my own boat, let alone set sail with a stowaway on board."

Tarik scowled. "It's probably part of the plot. To convince me I can trust you."

"What plot?"

"Oh don't pretend you don't know. I picked up enough of the signal to know that something was going down soon. Something that involved you. Something that involved a bomb."

The Monster paled under his tan. "A b-bomb?"

"Yes, a bomb." Tarik ignored the pounding in his head and leaned forward. "If you tell me about it now, I'll argue for taking the death penalty off the table."

"Just one bloody minute." The Monster stood, and Tarik's heart fluttered faster. "I have nothing to do with a plot. For all I know, *you're* the one with the plot."

Tarik scoffed, hoping like hell the Monster was buying his attitude as confidence. "Right. You're hardly good political extortion or ransom material, not with being out of the public eye for seventeen years."

For some reason, that seemed to hit home. The Monster sucked in a quick breath, and if Tarik didn't know better—if this weren't the fucking *Monster*—he'd swear the expression that chased across his face was hurt.

"A point, I suppose." He tossed the water pouch at Tarik, who caught it reflexively. "That's sealed. Drink it or not." He sent the little packet after the water and it landed on Tarik's damp thigh. "Acetaminophen. There's aspirin and ibuprofen in the first aid kit, if you prefer. But feel free to refuse it all and indulge your headache if that makes you happy." The Monster took the two strides necessary to reach the companionway and snatched up a metal bucket.

Tarik was tempted to scorn the water, just to prove he could, but his throat was so dry he thought he might possibly be mummified. So he cracked open the seal and guzzled a third of it, then wiped his mouth with the back of his hand. *Ugh.* His cuticles were tinged with red, the result of lolling around on a deck awash with wine. Which made very little sense no matter what the terms of his kidnapping were.

"Why is your deck awash in wine?"

The Monster paused with one foot on the first rung of the ladder. "It's not only wine. It's water too." He pointed to the boulder. "From the starboard water tank. At the moment, I care rather more about that than about whether you decide to get over yourself."

"Why am I not surprised," Tarik drawled. "Of course you'd care more about your precious yacht than about anybody's life—mine or whoever's being targeted by your bomb."

The Monster took his foot off the ladder and whirled, the bucket clanging against a bulkhead. "Listen, *Your Grace*, the port water tank has very little in it, and since there are two of us stranded here, the emergency supplies I was counting on will only last half as long." He jabbed a finger at Tarik.

"And for your information, I built this boat myself, so yes I care about it. I care that it was stolen from its dock and somehow transported at speeds it was never intended for and wrecked on a deserted island."

"How do you know it's deserted if you didn't plan to bring me here to begin with?"

"I know because I *looked*. We're on one of the uninhabited islands north of Crete. There are dozens of uninhabited islands in the Aegean."

"North of *Crete*? Fuck." Tarik pressed his fingers against his eyes. "How long was I out?"

"I don't know that, since the last time I saw you, you were definitely conscious." The Monster's tone said *"and annoying"* better than words.

"So how do you know where we are?" Because as Tarik glanced around, he couldn't spot a radio or anything resembling a navigation system.

"I just do. Some of the islands are privately owned, and I've visited them before. Unfortunately, we didn't get beached on one of those."

"Crete?" Tarik frowned, the pain in his head and the residual muzziness from the drug making him extraordinarily slow-witted. "But that's three-quarters of the way across the Mediterranean from the Abarran coast."

"Exactly." The Monster turned and climbed the ladder, disappearing out the hatch.

"Wait a minute." Tarik scrambled to his feet and nearly retched. He held it in, thanks to another swig of water. He glanced at the packet of pills in his hand. "Oh, what the hell." He downed them and followed the Monster onto the deck. The sun reflecting off white sands nearly blinded him, and he steadied himself on the cabin roof.

The Monster was standing next to the steering wheel—what did Tarik's yachting friends call it? *Ah, the helm. I need to remember the fucking lingo, or he'll know he's got an advantage over me.* He was staring at something behind the boat—*astern, ha!*—with a look of such intense sorrow that Tarik had a moment of uncertainty. *Could I be wrong about him?*

Tarik snorted, wincing when the simple rush of air through his sinuses caused another pulse of pain. *Nah. Even if I'm wrong, seventeen years' worth of other opinions couldn't possibly be.*

He staggered toward the rear—*stern, damn it*—to stare at the vast expanse of sand between the boat and the sea. He wasn't a sailor, not like some of his cousins who lived closer to the harbor, but even he knew that you couldn't land a ship this far from the water.

"How the fuck did we get here?"

The Monster shot him a disgusted glance. "You tell me. You're the one with the conspiracy theories."

Tarik scowled. "It's not a theory. I intercepted a message. Two of them."

"Then you should know all about it."

Tarik turned his head to escape the combination of hurt and contempt in those blue eyes and gazed out to sea. Which was exactly the same color. *Fuck.* "They were partial messages."

"So you don't know what's happening either?"

Tarik sat heavily atop a locker on the left—*grrr, port*—side of the boat, because it was a fair cop. "Not exactly. So why don't you tell me how you managed to sail your boat across ten meters of sand and fetch up against a rock?"

"I didn't." The Monster's eyebrows bunched. "It was the damnedest thing. The vandals cut the mooring rope"—his scowl deepened—"with my own bloody ax." He shot a wide-eyed glance at Tarik. "It wasn't actually *bloody*. I mean, with blood on it—"

"Fine. I get it." Tarik circled his hand in a *go-on* motion.

The Monster jerked a nod, his scowl returning. "Not a minute later, *Askatasun* got lifted at least ten meters into the air on this weird column of water and got swallowed in a fog bank. Then the water column launched us at what felt like light speed for approximately forever until it wrecked us here. I'm guessing we ended up so far from the waterline because the column dissipated when it hit the sand and the wave broke here."

Tarik's mouth had fallen open as soon as the Monster mentioned the mysterious water column. He snapped his teeth together, anger finally getting the better of his panic. *And thank fuck for that.* "Stormsurge."

The Monster glanced at him. "There wasn't a storm. Other than the fog and the speed-induced wind, it was more or less clear."

"No. Stormsurge is the power moniker of a supo who can manipulate ocean water—and any weather that's associated with it. You're lucky he didn't decide to add a monsoon for good measure." Tarik stared at the glassy sea. "But I expect that wasn't part of the contract. He charges a lot for that kind of shit."

"So this is a North Abarran plot after all, then." The Monster took a step toward Tarik. "We have treaties— ancient treaties, sacred treaties—that explicitly prevent Royals from taking supo contracts against the other country. This amounts to an act of war."

"Don't get your knickers in a twist. Stormsurge isn't an Abarran Royal of either country. He's unaffiliated. From Trinidad, I think. So any contracts he takes are technically neutral. Although if a Royal on either side was the contractee, then you're right. It's an act of aggression at the very least."

The Monster's expression was comical in its outrage. "How can he do that? Doesn't he care about property destruction? That people could get hurt? That people could *die*?"

"From what I've heard of him, he cares about the oceans. He's a marine biologist in his mundane job. In fact, he doesn't take many supo contracts at all, so whoever brought him in on this one must have paid big bucks. Probably enough to fund a new marine sanctuary or one of his other pet projects. But just involving Stormsurge for this much meant somebody with deep pockets is involved."

"I still don't see how—"

"None of the unaffiliated supos are bound by the laws of Abarra, North or South." Tarik chuckled mirthlessly. "Sometimes I envy them. And I'm damn sure there are a lot of non-Royals running around both our countries who have supo blood, given how impossible it was for our ancestors to keep it in their pants." He shrugged. "It's their bad luck to live in a country that outlaws powers for anybody but acknowledged Royals."

"I suppose. But I still think Stormsurge's behavior is irresponsible, bordering on criminal."

This time Tarik's laugh was louder, because how could this guy be so naïve? He was the *Monster of Roses*, for fuck's sake. "You find a court anywhere outside Abarra that'll prosecute a supo. The rest of the world likes to pretend we don't exist. In fact, we're only allowed to exist in our own countries because the pain in the ass Ministry of Powers keeps such a tight rein over us." Tarik rubbed his temples. Didn't help. "Register all supos. Submit to assessment when powers manifest. No exercising powers unless by contract. Blah blah blah."

"Whatever." The Monster tossed his bucket onto the sand. "But I'm billing this Stormsurge joker for my boat repairs." He jumped down next to the bucket.

A spike of alarm rocked Tarik to his feet. "Where are you going?"

The Monster picked up his bucket. "To find water."

"We've got water." Tarik brandished his pouch.

"Not enough for both of us. I was bringing a new supply onboard, and planning to fill the integrated water tanks, but that plan got derailed when your friend Stormsurge shanghaied me."

"He's not my friend."

The Monster tossed Tarik a sardonic look over his shoulder. "Then maybe I won't bill you for repairs too. Because as you so graciously pointed out, it's unlikely that his target was me. Somebody else put you on my boat a day before I was supposed to be on it. So as far as I'm concerned —plot or no plot, conspiracy or no conspiracy—this is all your fault."

CHAPTER FIVE

"Shit." Shoulders slumped, Sander stood at the edge of a precipice, staring at the picturesque waterfall tumbling over a rocky outcropping high overhead, a rainbow glistening in its spray as it plunged into the sea. The chasm that separated him from the falls was maybe five or six meters wide, but it might as well be five *kilo*meters, because he couldn't find any way to cross it. *And no way to scale that freaking sheer cliff either.*

He'd spend the last two hours surveying the island, scrambling far enough up one scrub-covered hillside to see its full extent.

The island wasn't big, maybe three square kilometers sporting nothing but rocks and dust-dimmed bushes—not a tree in sight. Sander supposed he should be grateful to Stormsurge, whoever the mercenary bastard was, that he'd managed to wreck them on the only stretch of sand in the whole place. Other than the beach where *Askatasun* lay, the rest of the coast was all sheer cliffs reminiscent of Montecristo. A little further to the north or south, and they'd be nothing but matchsticks floating on the tide right now.

He glared at the falls again, the only water source he'd been able to locate. Which was worse—discovering that the island where you were marooned with your enemy had no fresh water? Or discovering inaccessible fresh water with the enemy still part of the picture?

A tossup.

But the bottom line was still *no more water*, and at this time of year, significant rainfall was highly unlikely. He shaded his eyes and scanned the cerulean sky. It was completely clear—not a cloud, not a bird, not even a distant contrail. *At this point, I'd even be grateful for a glimpse of Otho's ridiculous yellow cape.*

As he picked his way down the hill, he mentally inventoried the contents of the emergency kit. It had started out with a dozen five-ounce water pouches, but he'd already given Arles one. That wasn't a lot for the two of them, but they only needed to last for a week, less if Katalin resolved the elephant crisis and got back from Tanzania sooner.

What am I thinking? Even if the crisis was resolved, Katalin wouldn't be able to resist hanging out with the elephants as long as possible. He'd just have to hold on until she was back in touch with her gossipy seagulls.

Sander hopped down off the last bit of hillside, his belly swooping when his ankle rolled in the soft sand. *Pay attention, idiot.* The last thing he needed was to be incapacitated on top of being thirsty. *A week. That's all. I can handle a week.* They had shelter in *Askatasun*'s cabin and fish in the sea for food. They'd manage.

He squared his shoulders, but when he faced *Askatasun*, listing a bit to starboard halfway down the beach, his throat closed and he dashed a hand across his eyes. His poor *Askatasun*, her sleek hull splintered, her rudder torn off, her keel buried deep in sand and probably compromised six different ways.

I'll fix you. Don't worry. As soon as we're found, I'll make sure we take you home and I'll fix every single thing. Once Katalin finds out—

He slapped his forehead. His luggage. The handcart on the dock. The open marina door. When the crew arrived to find *Askatasun* gone but without her provisions, surely they'd contact the Manor. Luken, with his usual scary efficiency, would contact Katalin and *boom*, problem solved. In fact, help might already be on the way.

But do I want to bet my life on it? More to the point, do I want to bet Arles's life on it?

Sander scowled as he trudged toward *Askatasun*, his mood not improved by the sand sifting into his deck shoes. *If I had to get trapped on a deserted island with somebody, why did it have to be* him? He'd been so horrible to poor Merrick, and then to blame Sander for their predicament when he'd only been trying to help? *Not the Duke of Arles. More like the Duke of Arse.* He was probably the reason they were here in the first place.

As Sander neared the boat, he spotted something dark flapping on the gunwale. He slowed. Was that… Yes. A pair of trousers. And a jacket. Did that mean… His heart beat in his throat as he crept toward the water, craning his neck to peer past *Askatasun*'s stern.

And tripped over his feet, nearly face-planting in the sand. Because the Duke of Arles was standing knee deep in the surf. Naked. Naked and bent over as he swished his hands through the water.

Sander gulped. *Duke of Arse indeed.*

The bucket clanged against Sander's kneecap and Arles looked over his shoulder. Then he… Sander's mouth dried like a beached flounder because Arles *turned around*.

Oh my God. Arles's skin was that same lovely brown *all over*, his chest lightly furred with dark hair, a tantalizing line extending down to the nest of dark curls around his cock. And although said cock was soft against Arles's thigh, it was nevertheless… *gah!*

As Arles splashed to shore, wringing sea water out of what must be his shirt, Sander's gaze slid to *Askatasun*. He'd been so complacent about not needing to build a shelter, but the wreck had destroyed the guest bunk.

There's only one berth.

The bucket rattled in Sander's trembling hand as Arles stopped and shook out his shirt. He gave it a disgusted glare—unless that look was intended for Sander. "Can we call off this farce now?"

Sander was struck momentarily speechless. *I have a voice. I know words.* He cleared his throat. "I'm sorry. What?"

"This." Arles snapped the shirt at *Askatasun*. "This ridiculous charade that we're lost at sea. Castaway with only each other to depend on. That's what this is about, right? Payback?"

"No." *Don't ogle his body. Don't ogle his body.* He tossed the bucket aside, damn its telltale rattle, and climbed into *Askatasun's* cockpit. He lifted the lid on the starboard storage locker and rummaged under the life vests. *Aha. Thank goodness I don't let the crew clear out my old board shorts.* He'd learned that on one sail when his only pair had gotten blown overboard. He pulled out a faded blue pair. "Here. In case you don't want a sunburned..." He flapped the shorts in the general direction of Arles's groin before balling them up and tossing them over the gunwale.

Arles caught them, staring down at them as if he'd never seen such things before.

Damn. I've got spare shorts, but no spare shirts. He sighed and shed his windbreaker so he could strip off his T-shirt. "This has UV protection, and there's sunblock in the medicine locker." He tossed the shirt after the shorts, but it fell to the sand because Arles didn't even try to catch it.

Instead, he was staring up at Sander, lips parted, an unreadable expression on his face. He shut his mouth with an audible click of his teeth and picked up the shirt. "Thank you."

"You're welcome." Sander put his windbreaker back on and opened the port storage locker. *Thank God.* His fishing tackle was still there. Apparently the vandals either hadn't known about it, hadn't had time to finish the job, or else their intent hadn't been Arles's death. Even though he'd tossed that accusation at Arles from pure temper, now that he thought about it, the attack *had* to be against the Duke. Sander wasn't supposed to be on deck until tomorrow. *But why choose my boat for the attack? What does it all mean?*

Arles climbed aboard, thankfully wearing the shorts and shirt, even though the way the shirt stretched tight over his chest was still a distraction. Sander averted his eyes and retrieved the battered green metal tackle box.

"Is that where you've hidden the radio?"

Sander glanced up at him. "I don't have a radio on board."

Arles glared at him. "Why the fuck not? Isn't that like a maritime law or something?"

"Special dispensation for Abarran Royals." Even ones that don't have manageable powers. Or maybe because of it. Maybe the Ministry of Transportation was as eager to get rid of Sander as the rest of his countrymen.

"I can't believe I'm stuck on a deserted island with an idiot who doesn't have a radio on his boat," Arles muttered.

"Hold this." Sander shoved the tackle box into Arles's hands and bent to free the fly rod from its bracket. "And be thankful you're stuck on a deserted island with an idiot who has a fishing pole."

"Why do we need that?"

"Because we were boat-jacked before I loaded my provisions on board. I told you that. We've got a few emergency rations in the kit, but they're not exactly gourmet fare, and I prefer to consider them a last resort. So if you don't want to fast for a week until rescue arrives, I need to catch some fish."

"Oops." Arles smirked, fingers drumming a tattoo on the metal box. "You just admitted your guilt."

"I didn't because I'm not guilty!"

"Then how do you know how long we'll be here? It's over, Roses. Why not own your fuck-up and call for help?"

Sander closed the locker and set the rod on top, then snatched the tackle box from Arles and glared at him. "Why don't *you*?"

"Because I don't have my fucking cell phone." Arles jabbed a forefinger at Sander, although it didn't touch his chest. "*You* decreed I couldn't bring it with me to our meeting. I guess now I know why."

Sander huffed out an exasperated breath. "Take a look around you, *Your Grace*. Do you really think a cell phone would do you any good here? The nearest cell tower is sixty kilometers away!"

Arles's eyes narrowed in suspicion. "So you claim to have no part in kidnapping me, yet you know where we are. Like *that* isn't a giveaway to your complicity."

"I know where we are because I..." Actually, Sander couldn't articulate why he always knew where he was once he got out onto the water, away from the incessant thrum of civilization. He'd always chalked it up to familiarity with the waters he sailed, but he'd never been this far east, at least not by himself. *On the other hand, Arles doesn't know that.* "Because I've been sailing the Mediterranean since I was a boy." He pointed northwest. "The Greek mainland is that way, the Aegean Islands are north and east. Several of those islands are privately owned and developed."

"Just not this one." Arles's tone was edged sarcasm. "Convenient."

Sander set the tackle box down with a *clang*. "For God's sake, you're acting like I'm not stuck here too. Like there's not a giant hole in my boat's hull. Like most of my water supply and at least one keg of wine aren't washing around below deck. You're freaking *Wavelength. You* call for help."

For the first time since he'd woken in the cabin, Arles looked uneasy. "I... I can't."

"Why not? According to word on the street, you're like a perpetual eye in the sky. Well, ear in the sky, I suppose." Sander folded his arms across his chest. "I've heard their nickname for you is Eavesdropper."

Arles scowled as though he was actually offended. *Unbelievable.* "I don't listen to everything. There's way too much of it. If I don't block it out, it gives me a migraine."

Despite his annoyance, Sander was intrigued. "So how do you block it out?"

Arles snorted. "As if you didn't know."

Sander heaved an enormous sigh and let his arms fall to his sides. "I'm sorry to wound your giant ego, *Your Grace,* but I don't spend my days devouring stories about you in the newspapers."

"Prefer to do your stalking online, do you?"

Sander stiffened. "I don't go online."

"Right." Arles turned away, his jaw working. "Of all the bullshit you've spouted, that one takes the prize."

"It's not bullshit! I can't be around electronics without frying them." Sander spread his hands to encompass *Askatasun.* "That's why I navigate using a sextant and a chronometer." Or used to. He rarely used them anymore. "That's why I built *Askatasun* with mechanical rather than electronic controls. That's why there's no radio on board." He propped his fists on his hips. "That's the honest to God truth. Now will you stop taking the piss and tell me why you can't send a freaking SOS?"

Arles pressed his lips together, eyes narrowed as if he were about to tell Sander to go to hell—again—but then he laughed and held his arms wide. "Because of this. Because we're on a fucking island that's barely as big as the New Palace. My powers don't work when I'm surrounded by water." He lowered himself onto the starboard locker. "The only time I get any relief at home is when I'm in the bath." He smiled, a wry upturn of his lips that sent an unexpected jolt of *want* down Sander's spine. "You should see my custom-built tubs. Since I spend as much time in them as I can, they're what you might call over the top."

Sander sat down gingerly on the port locker. "I think that might be the first true thing you've told me. The first real thing."

Arles shrugged. "Seemed fair, considering you'd just spilled your big secret."

Sander frowned out at the horizon, the hump of another island barely visible. "So whoever planned this had to know about your weakness."

Arles drew himself up, chin raised haughtily. "It's not a weakness."

"No?" Sander grinned. "What would you call it? A *feature?*"

There was that smile again. "Okay, so it's a weakness. But a lot of people know about it." He inclined his head to Sander. "Other than South Abarran princes, apparently, who prefer to do their crossword puzzles by hand."

Tarik picked at the frayed edge of the shorts the Monster had lent him. *Maybe I should stop referring to him as the Monster. He's got a name.* Besides, Tarik was starting to believe this whole affair might be bigger than both of them.

He gestured to the empty bucket. "Didn't find water?"

"Oh, I found it, all right."

The Monster jumped onto the sand again and picked up what Tarik recognized as the boat's rudder. Well, former rudder, because it was split halfway up the middle and a huge chunk was missing from the top—a chunk that was still attached to the stern.

"Then why not bring some back, if you're so concerned about it?"

The Monster stalked down the beach a ways and tossed the rudder onto the sand. "Because I can't reach it. It's a waterfall tumbling over a sheer cliff face about five meters across a chasm that plunges straight into the sea." He shot Tarik a speculative look. "I don't suppose you're hiding a secret second power? Because it would be really useful if you could fly like my cousin Otho."

"Even if I did, I never admit it. Is that part of your plan? Prove I'm violating the supo laws so you can discredit me?"

The Monster stalked to where the boulder had become one with the boat and started pulling off splintered pieces of the hull, tossing them into the pile with the rudder. "For the last time, I have nothing to do with you being here. But you know what I think?" He turned, a long, wickedly pointed piece of wood in his hand, jabbing it in Tarik's direction. "I'm convinced this was an attack against you—"

"You think?"

Tarik's dry comment surprised the Monster into a short laugh. And good lord, when his eyes lit up with mirth, when his full lips curved like that, white teeth flashing in his tanned skin, he was one of the most beautiful men Tarik had ever seen—and he'd seen the cream of the crop. All of them had paraded in front of him at one of Bastien's interminable courtship parties at one point or another, part of his incurably romantic cousin's attempts to turn a political alliance into a love match. Despite Bastien's best efforts, Tarik had never felt a twinge of anything more than mild liking for any of them.

If the Monster had been at one of those parties, though...

He shook his head impatiently, a damp curl clinging to one cheek. This was the *Monster of Roses*, for fuck's sake. If he wasn't the outright enemy of Tarik's country, then he was at least the main competitor of his vineyard. He was the very last man on earth Tarik should be attracted to.

But as the Monster glared at the boulder, the hands on his hips framing his world-class ass, a twinge of regret unfurled in Tarik's chest. *Then again, right here, right now? Other than me, he's the* only *man on earth.*

The Monster huffed and strode to the stern to climb into the boat again.

"What are you doing?" Tarik asked.

He paused in the companionway. "Most of the broken boards are inside. We might as well use them to build a signal fire."

"Will that even work? For that matter, aren't most ships made of fiberglass?"

"Most are. But I built this one myself. It's wooden, and even treated wood will burn eventually. I'm not willing to dismantle the whole boat though, so we'll mostly need to use the driftwood from the beach." He pointed at the bleached wood scattered along the sand like the bones of dinosaurs who'd made poor sunbathing choices. Sorrow flickered across his face. "But it's not like the hull scraps are good for anything now. I'll have to rebuild that section with new timber once we get home."

"Why do we need a signal fire?"

The Monster blinked at him, one hand on the cabin roof. "That should be fairly obvious. This island is uninhabited, but the seas around here aren't exactly empty." He pointed to the southeast. "You can just see another island on the horizon. If *Askatasun* were seaworthy and the wind cooperated, we could sail there in less than a day." He laughed again, softly, as if to himself, and Tarik was glad of the shorts. Because if he'd still been naked, his traitorous dick would have betrayed his highly inappropriate interest. "Of course, if *Askatasun* were seaworthy, we could sail home." He straightened his shoulders. "But she's not. So if we can attract the attention of a passing boat or plane, we'll get off this island all the sooner."

He disappeared below deck, and a muffled curse drifted after him, as well as the sound of splashing. *Right.* The cabin deck was awash in watered wine. *My suit didn't absorb it all, even though it sure as fuck felt like it.*

Tarik leaned on the gunwale, studying the wood pile made from pieces of the Monster's boat. *A boat he built himself.* When you created something like this, something beautiful—and even though Tarik wasn't a sailing aficionado, he could admit that the boat was beautiful, with its sleek hull painted a glossy midnight blue and the golden brown wood of the deck and cabin gleaming in the sunlight —seeing it damaged was like a kick in the gut. And yet the Monster was willing to burn parts of something he clearly loved for a better chance at rescue.

Yes, it meant rescue for the Monster, but for Tarik too. And if he was going to this much trouble, maybe they really were stranded.

And maybe Tarik needed to cut the guy some slack.

But not too much. Because Tarik couldn't forget the message fragment that named the Monster in connection with a bomb. He crossed the cockpit and peered through the hatch.

The Monster was holding two flat pieces of red-painted wood which, judging from the way he was trying to fit their jagged ends together, used to be one. "So much for my collapsible dinghy," he muttered. He tossed the pieces onto a tarp he'd laid across a fold-down table. He didn't acknowledge Tarik—just turned back and wrenched a splintered board off the hull with a *crack* and a grunt.

Tarik cleared his throat. "What else needs doing?"

"We need"—*grunt*—"kindling. Cut up the"—*grunt*— "driftwood." The liberated board joined the others on the tarp. "The vandals took my ax, but the emergency kit in the bow storage locker has a hand saw of some kind." He wiped his forehead with the back of his hand and Tarik admired the play of the muscles in his forearms. *Apparently I'm an arm man. Who knew?*

"Uh huh. What else?"

"We'll need something to make an SOS in the sand. Rocks. Big rocks."

"Of course we do. How big are we talking?" Tarik nodded at the boulder protruding into the cabin. "Not the size of that one, I presume."

The Monster glared at him for an instant before wry humor flickered across his face. "Only as big as your head. Of course, if you'll have trouble carrying anything *that* large, I can handle it and you can build the fire."

"I can carry a few fucking rocks," Tarik growled. *You're not the only competent one on this island.* But who was Tarik trying to convince? Himself or the Monster?

"Not a few. A lot. The SOS should be at least three meters tall."

"What about food? Surely that's a bit of a priority too."

"Fish won't be biting again until later in the day. If you're feeling peckish—" There was that glint of amusement in the Monster's eyes again. "—there are some truly delightful emergency rations in the pack."

"I can wait," Tarik grumbled. He backed away from the companionway and turned toward the locker. "I can wait just as long as you can." He jumped down onto the sand. The impact raised a little flare of pain at the base of his skull, but nothing approaching his usual headaches. He counted it a win.

Rocks. Rocks. Rocks as big as my head. He scoured the beach, but it held a dearth of rocks. By the time the Monster climbed onto the deck and lowered his laden tarp over the side, Tarik was irritable, sweaty, desperately craving a half gallon of ice water—and had amassed only enough rocks for the first curve of the first S.

He glared up at the Monster who'd just emerged on deck toting a neon orange duffel that Tarik assumed was the famous emergency kit. "This fucking beach *has* no rocks. If you wanted to torture me with hard labor, you should have kidnapped me to a different island."

"For the last time—" The Monster dropped the kit and jumped to the sand, "I didn't kidnap you. You stowed away on my boat."

"It wasn't exactly my idea."

"It wasn't mine either."

"So you say."

The Monster sighed and plucked one of the red scraps off the tarp. "Use these along with the rocks. They're bright enough to show up against the white sand, and we've got enough driftwood that we don't need them for the fire."

"Fine." Tarik snatched the arm-long board and added it to the S.

The Monster climbed back aboard and started unloading the emergency kit and lining its contents up on the locker behind the helm. "Aha!" He grinned in triumph, holding something aloft. "I knew it. A cable saw."

"Cable saw?"

"Like a hand-held chain saw. We can use this to cut the driftwood into manageable chunks."

"Whatever," Tarik muttered. "Although it would be a lot easier on both of us if you'd just give in and call your fucking accomplices."

As Tarik bent over to heft another rock, something whizzed past his shoulder and hit the wood scrap with a *thwack*.

He rose slowly, anger burning in his belly. "Did you just fucking *throw* something at me?" He turned, fists clenched, ready to launch into the fight that had been building between them since they'd first laid eyes on one another.

But the Monster wasn't glaring at Tarik with anger or hate or triumph. He was staring at his own hands, his expression one of utter horror.

Tarik glanced behind him. There, glinting against the cheerful red paint, was a foot of heavy steel chain—embedded in the board as if it had been shot from a fucking cannon.

CHAPTER SIX

Sander started to tremble, his teeth chattering. *How did I — What did I— If I'd hit Arles, he'd be—*

"What the fuck?" Arles's tone was sharp, angry. *He has every right.* "Is this what you do? Fling metal about? I thought your specialty was killing electronics?"

"I don't know. I never—" Sander's knees folded, and he butt-planted on the deck. He buried his face in his hands, chest heaving as he tried not to pass out.

Dimly, he heard Arles climb aboard. Heard a muffled curse. *I can't blame him. Hell, I wouldn't blame him if he knocked me cold, or worse.*

But instead, a hand pressed to Sander's back. "Here. Drink this."

Sander shook his head, folding further into himself.

"Damn it, Roses. It's fucking hot out here, and you've been heaving wood about when you haven't been marching around the island. And when you gave me water, I didn't see you take any for yourself. So you've got to be dehydrated."

Sander raised his head. Arles was holding one of the pouches from the emergency pack in front of him. "I shouldn't. We don't know—"

"Just drink the damn water."

So Sander did, although when it hit his belly, he was afraid it would reverse course. But Arles was right. He needed it. So he made himself sip slowly, and the black spots in his vision gradually receded. When he was done, Arles took the pouch from his limp fingers and sat down on the lazarette next to the emergency pack.

He braced his elbows on his knees, clasped his hands together, and gazed into Sander's eyes, his expression grim. "We need to talk."

"I'm sorry. I'm so sorry. I didn't—"

"Not about that. Or not exactly. Did you intend to impale me with the cable saw?"

"What? No! Of course not. I don't know how it happened."

"No? I think I can guess. The whole frying electronics thing. The way your touch—" He cleared his throat. "Magnetism."

Sander could do nothing but blink at him stupidly. "Magnetism?"

"Roses— Sorry, what's your name again?"

"Alesander. Sander."

"Sander, then. I'm Tarik. Look, I know your reputation."

Sander huffed. "Who doesn't?"

Arles—no, Tarik waved Sander's words away. "Did the Ministry of Powers assess you? Did they try to figure out *why* you fry electronics?"

"How? Every time they got near me with their monitoring equipment—" He spread his fingers in jazz hands. "*Pffzzzt.*"

Tarik carded his fingers through his curls. "Fuck. The Ministry is such a bag of dicks. If their modern tech didn't work, why didn't they go old school?"

"Old school?"

"Yep. Old school." Tarik sat up and frowned as he poked at the contents of the emergency kit. "What were you doing before you launched the saw at me?"

"Nothing. I mean, I was just standing there. I'd taken the saw out of its packet and had unrolled it."

"So you were holding it in both hands?"

Sander tried to remember, pushing against the roiling guilt and horror that clouded his brain. "Yes. I was testing the length."

Tarik smiled—a wry upturn of his full lips, the first time he'd looked at Sander with anything but anger, contempt, or derision—and Sander had to catch his breath. "And then I spouted another asshole comment, didn't I?"

"Um…"

"You don't have to pull your punches. I know what I can be like. I'm sorry."

Sander frowned. "Why apologize to me? I'm the one that nearly nailed you with a chain missile. And last I checked, you were still sure I'd lured you into getting conked on the head and drugged for the privilege of stowing away on my boat as part of my wicked plan for vineyard domination."

"Because…" Tarik sighed. "Because I've finally gotten my head out of my own ass and admitted that we're both in this together. It doesn't matter whose idea it was or whose fault. We have to soldier on until it's over, one way or another." He shrugged. "And maybe I can recognize remorse when I see it. You clearly didn't want to hurt me, despite what was undoubtedly extreme provocation. So… truce?" He held out his right hand.

Sander wrapped his arms across his belly. "Are you sure you want to touch me? I mean—"

"I'm sure." Tarik kept his hand extended, so Sander tentatively closed his around it—and took his first truly free breath in what felt like forever.

Tarik didn't release Sander's hand right away. Instead, he turned it over and traced a finger over Sander's callused palm, eliciting a shiver. "You work with your hands."

Sander nodded. "Woodworking and blacksmithing mostly. I shoe my mare. All our horses, really."

"And build your own boat." Tarik held out his other hand. "May I?" Sander nodded again, releasing his death grip on his stomach to lay his palm against Tarik's.

The tingle that traveled up Sander's arm at the touch zoomed all the way to his balls and he stifled a gasp.

"A magnet has two poles. North—" Tarik lifted Sander's right hand. "—and south." He lifted the left and smiled again. "Kind of like Abarra. North and South, always at odds, never able to get close because their forces are opposite. Repelling each other. But if you reverse one of them—" He laced the fingers of his left hand with Sander's right. "—you make a connection. A bond."

"Is that what..." Sander swallowed. "Is that what we're doing here?"

"I'm pretty sure we have no choice." He let go of Sander's hand, and Sander swallowed a protest at the loss. "But we're not talking about that right now."

Sander's heart sank. "We're not?"

"No." He gripped Sander's wrists instead. "We're talking about the power, the magnetic force, that's generated between *your* north and south poles."

Sander snatched his hands away. "You saw what happened. I could have killed you, or at least injured you badly. I can't control it. It's a rogue power."

Tarik reached out and gently grasped Sander's wrists again, his movements and attitude polar—*heh*—opposites from his earlier hostility. "It's not a rogue power. It's an *untrained* power. Fuck, it took me years before I could filter out the noise in the airwaves and concentrate on a single message. You can't be expected to control your powers unless you practice. And if those idiots at the Ministry of Powers couldn't be bothered to try to understand it, how could you? You were a kid when it manifested, right?"

Sander nodded. "Ten."

Tarik shook his head, clucking his tongue. "Such a tragedy. A ten-year-old kid unable to play video games."

Sander was surprised into a laugh. "I admit, I mourned the loss. My sister and I held a state funeral for my Gameboy and buried it next to the lake."

"And then what? You just avoided technology for the rest of your life?"

Sander's belly filled with ice. *Except once.* "It seemed like the safest path."

"Safe, my ass. More like the laziest path for those Ministry assholes." Tarik stood up and pulled Sander to his feet. "Now I'm a lot of things, but lazy isn't one of them, and since you built your own fucking boat with no power tools? I'm guessing it's not one of your failings either." He turned back to the emergency kit, snatched up a Swiss Army knife, and unfolded one of the blades. "Take this in both hands."

"What?" Instead, Sander retreated until he bumped into the helm, hands clasped behind him. "I can't. What if I stab you?"

Tarik advanced on him. "So what? I'm the enemy, right?" He raised a sardonic brow, holding the knife out and waggling it with the blade parallel to Sander's chest. "Unless you're afraid an injured Duke of Arles will be less valuable for your ransom demands."

Disappointment warred with annoyance in Sander's middle. "You said you'd gotten over that notion." He jabbed both forefingers at Tarik, staying well clear of the knife, because who knew what would happen. "If you don't think—"

Tarik let go of the knife and just for a moment, it hovered in the air, suspended between Sander's hands. Sander stared at it, blood draining from his head. Then it clattered to the deck.

Tarik spread his palms. "See? Magnetic force." He scooped the knife up and gestured for Sander to precede him. "Now let's get off the boat and set up a nice safe target in the sand for you to practice your knife throwing skills."

"Are you crazy? Do you know what I'm capable of?"

"No." Tarik crowded up against him, and Sander's breath got lost somewhere south of his throat. "And neither do you, which is the whole fucking point. Don't you think it's time to find out? Besides..." He spread his arms and stepped back. "What else have we got to do?"

"Other than make a signal fire, finish the SOS, catch fish for dinner—"

"I'll handle the fire and the SOS. As for fish, if we don't get to them tonight, they'll still be there tomorrow, and as you mentioned, we've got a lovely selection of—" He angled his head, peering at the kit's scattered contents. "—emergency food rations. Full of vitamins and minerals." He waggled his eyebrows and tapped one of the vacuum-sealed packets. "It says so. Right there." He straightened, his expression morphing from playful to determined. "So stop stalling, Sander. It's time to take charge of your destiny." He pointed imperiously to port.

"Yeah, yeah. Big talk," Sander muttered, but he jumped to the sand because if he stayed that close to Tarik for another instant, he'd be tempted to form another bond—between their lips. "Bet you're a huge hit at political rallies."

"I avoid those whenever possible." Tarik followed Sander over the transom. "Too many texts and tweets and radio feeds. Gives me a monster headache." He froze. "Er, sorry."

"Don't worry about it." Sander retrieved the largest piece of *Askatasun*'s rudder. "I'm used to it."

"Maybe. But you shouldn't have to be." Tarik grabbed one handle of the captive chain saw, braced his foot on the board, and yanked. "Damn, Sander. You really pack a punch." He grasped the other handle and eased it back and forth until the saw teeth bit and he could work it free. "Just make sure you don't aim it at me next time."

Tarik winked and strolled across the sand toward the largest tumble of driftwood, his arms below the T-shirt sleeves as smooth and brown as *Askatasun*'s decks in the sun, his borrowed shorts stretched tight across his ass—which gave Sander's cock ideas about exactly what he'd prefer to aim at Tarik.

God, I'm pathetic. He doesn't even like *me.* He paused, the rudder under his arm. *Do I* like *him?* Tarik Jaso, Duke of Arles, was an arrogant, hot-tempered, self-described asshole with an ego the size of Castle Abarra and powers that made him a by-word on the streets. On the other hand, he wasn't stupid. *So if he thinks I stand a chance of succeeding…*

Sander wedged the rudder upright in the sand. *But even if I fail spectacularly, he's right. It's past time for me to take control of my own destiny.*

Tarik kept one eye on Sander as he hauled driftwood and sawed it into reasonably sized pieces. Occasionally, a curse would waft across the sand, but for the most part, Sander was quiet, focused, and—if the occasional *thunk*s were any indication—actually making progress.

Tarik felt only half guilty for goading Sander into experimenting with his powers. The guilty half acknowledged that the man was obviously terrified he'd do something unforgivable. The other half, despite the words he'd spouted earlier, still couldn't discount that message fragment. He was certain Sander—or rather the Monster—was involved in some kind of planned terrorist attack. But as the perpetrator or the victim? The third half—God, Tarik hated fractions—was just bored with sitting on the beach waiting for rescue to arrive.

Bastien always accused him of being an adrenaline junkie, of deliberately seeking out conflict for the thrill of it, or creating his own if he couldn't find any. But he hadn't always been like this. When he was a boy, before his powers manifested, Bastien gave him just as much grief for hiding in some out-of-the-way corner of the New Palace with a book.

Afterward, though, his brain ceaselessly bombarded with the evidence of how truly appalling people could be to one another, he'd toughened the fuck up. He sighed and tossed another driftwood log onto the pile. What wouldn't he give to return to those days, before responsibilities, before the headaches, before the burden of everyone's secrets?

He frowned, coiling the cable saw into a loop. Now that he thought about it, other than the faint residual ache from where he'd been coshed—and thank goodness his kidnappers were lousy coshers—his head felt better than it had in years. Even when he was floating in one of his lovely bathtubs, the ache only receded to manageable levels. When was the last time he'd been free and clear?

Sander had mentioned that some of these islands were privately owned. *Maybe I should invest in one myself.* Although not this one. He was heartily sick of it already.

He climbed onto the boat and checked the emergency kit. It held some safety matches in a waterproof container. He peered inside. Not many. Was there another way to light the fire?

"Damn it!" Sander stomped across the sand and retrieved the knife. "I'm never going to get the hang of this."

"You're doing great," Tarik called. He held up the matches. "Is it okay to use these to light the fire?"

Sander shaded his eyes. "There's a flint lighter in the galley. Also a folding shovel in the lazarette. That's the storage locker aft of the helm."

"I know what a lazarette is." He didn't. "But why do I need a shovel?"

"You'll need to dig a pit for the fire."

"Of course I will," Tarik muttered.

"I can help." Sander scowled at the target. "I'm obviously not accomplishing much here."

"Nope. You keep working." He leaned over the gunwale. "Instead of trying for brute force, aim for finesse. Don't fling the knife at the target. Float it."

Sander stalked across the sand until he was directly below Tarik. "How am I supposed to do that? It won't be between my, er…" He stared down at his hands. "My poles."

Tarik couldn't help it—his gaze flicked down to Sander's package. *Stop thinking about his* other *pole.* "So? Magnetic fields don't have to be small. The earth's surrounded by one. Just make yours bigger. Control it. Don't let it control you."

Sander opened his mouth as if to snark back, but an arrested expression crossed his face and he stared down at his hands, flipping them palm up to palm down. Muttering to himself, he wandered back to his target.

"You're welcome," Tarik murmured, then retrieved the shovel and got busy digging a fucking pit.

He had to admit, though, that when he finally had the fire roaring, he felt a sense of accomplishment and the urge to pound on his chest. *I did this. I made fire.* Okay, he made it with a mechanical lighter, but he couldn't suppress the caveman response. *Oh, what the hell.* He glanced surreptitiously at Sander to make sure he wasn't looking and then punched the air with a silent shout.

He crossed his arms and contemplated it with satisfaction. He'd piled on some greener fuel from the stumpy bushes, figuring the smoke would be more visible in the daylight, but the wind snatched at it before it rose more than a couple of meters. Would it even be visible to anyone until after dark? Maybe he should have focused on the SOS first and left the fire for tonight.

He studied the position of the sun, still a hand span above the horizon. Fuck, how much longer could this day possibly get?

He got busy with the SOS and had just finished the O when Sander whooped.

"Tarik! Come quick!"

Tarik dropped the rock he was holding and raced as fast as he was able with the sand shifting under his bare feet. Sander was standing a couple of meters from the target, the knife in his hand. His grin rivaled the sun. "Watch this!"

With the blade safely tucked away, he held the knife between the thumb and forefinger of each hand. He bowed his head, the cords in his neck distended, and released his hold.

And the knife floated in the air.

"Good," Tarik began, "but—"

"Shhh!"

Before Tarik could retort that nobody *shhh*ed him, Sander opened his palms, widening his arms and made a gentle pushing motion. The knife floated forward for several feet. Then Sander shot his palms forward as if slapping an invisible wall and it sped through the air to thump against the rudder.

He turned a shining face to Tarik. "It's like you said. The field is manipulable. I can *feel* it now. It's everywhere. Under my feet. Up in the air. All around."

Tarik held up his fist for a bump. "You're totally the Magnet Man."

Sander chuckled. "Don't get carried away. I can levitate a knife a couple of meters. It's not like I've solved world peace." He scooped the knife out of the sand and smirked at Tarik. "Although it did get me out of building the fire."

"Smartass."

Sander's smirk vanished, and he stared down at his feet, toeing a line in the sand with one shoe. "I'm grateful that you got me to do this, Tarik, don't get me wrong. But I'm not sure what the point is. I probably should have helped you. Or gone fishing. Or swabbed out *Askatasun*'s cabin so we're not wading through wine tonight."

Tarik raised an eyebrow. "Why would we be wading through wine?"

"Since we've got *Askatasun*, and she's mostly intact, we don't need to build a shelter. We can sleep in her cabin. The wreck took out the guest bunk, so there's, um..." A flush tinted Sander's tan cheeks. "Only one berth. But—"

"Let's worry about sleeping arrangements later." Tarik took a step forward, trying to ignore the pulse of his very interested dick. "Can you really not see the point of this?"

"Other than keeping me out of your hair most of the afternoon?" Sander's gaze flicked to Tarik's hair, and he swallowed convulsively.

Oho. So he's got a thing for my hair, eh? Tarik ran a hand through his hair, slowly—except his curls were not exactly pristine right now, hardly in a state for slo-mo hair porn. *Back to the issue at hand.*

Tarik pointed to the bucket, abandoned by the boat's stern. "The point is that you can manipulate that bucket to reach the unreachable waterfall." He spread his palms. "Fresh water problem solved."

Sander's jaw sagged. "Are you serious? It's one thing to toss around a knife that weighs no more than a few grams, but a bucket full of water? I'm not that strong."

"You'll never know until you try. What have you got to lose?"

"Uh, the bucket."

"Stop whining." Tarik strode across the sand and retrieved the bucket, then returned and handed it to Sander. "Practice with this for a while. I've got an SOS to finish and a deck to swab."

And after that, I have to figure out how to survive tonight.

Because it wasn't a lethal midnight ambush by the legendary Monster of Roses that worried Tarik. It was how he could keep his hands off Sander Fiala while sleeping in the same fucking bed.

The kidnappers failed to do me in, but blue balls could be the death of me.

CHAPTER SEVEN

Despite the relative warmth of the night, despite his windbreaker, despite the roaring signal fire in front of them, Sander shivered, his gaze on the orange light flickering on *Askatasun*'s hull and that damned boulder. He took another tiny sip from his water pouch—*only six left*—the taste of the lemon-flavored emergency rations lingering on his tongue. *I'll definitely need to fish tomorrow.*

His belly quivered, and he ordered himself to calm down. *Like that ever works.* He took another sip because the rations wouldn't taste any better coming up than they did going down.

He wasn't sure if he was more nervous about tomorrow, when he'd have to challenge his barely leashed powers on a task that could mean survival and no doubt fail miserably. Or tonight, when he'd be sharing a not very spacious berth with the Duke of Arles, who hardly more than a day ago had faced him across the border with murder in his eye.

Who am I kidding? Of course *I'm more nervous about tonight.*

For one thing, tonight was *now*. Tomorrow was still off in the distance, and to get there, he had to make it through the next ten hours. He glanced sidelong at Tarik, who was gazing into the fire with the hint of a smile on his lips. The stress lines between his brows had gradually smoothed as night closed in around them. He'd even offered a mocking toast of *"Bon appétit,"* raising his water pouch to Sander over their emergency ration meal.

Could someone really go from hostile to helpful in the space of twenty-four hours? Because his treatment of poor Merrick was still fresh in Sander's memory. *But that was the Duke of Arles. This is* Tarik. And Tarik had been more patient with Sander's ineptitude than anyone other than his mother, sister, and valet. *A contradiction wrapped in a conundrum wrapped in a really, really hot body.*

The body in question pushed himself off the blanket they'd spread over the sand and tossed another log onto the fire. "There. Think that'll keep it going most of the night?"

Sander shrugged, trying—and failing—not to stare at Tarik's ass as he bent over to brush off his shins. "Probably not. I'll need to come out and stoke it once or twice."

Tarik studied him, the reflection of the flames dancing in his dark eyes. "I can split the duty with you. You don't have to do it all."

"It's all right. I'm used to rousing during the night while I'm at sea."

Tarik's grin flashed. "Not exactly at sea right now, are we?"

Sander flapped his hands, then remembered that his hands could do serious damage if he wasn't careful and tucked them in the windbreaker's pockets. "Same thing."

"Suit yourself." Tarik patted his belly. "Following that five-star gourmet meal, and after the day we've had, I'm more than ready to turn in." He glanced over his shoulder into the dark, where the breeze rustled through the bushes. "I felt much less intimidated by pissing in the underbrush when I could actually see it."

"You—" Sander laughed. He couldn't help it. "There's a composting toilet in *Askatasun*'s sea head. You don't have to use nature's facilities."

Tarik stared at him, jaw sagging, and Sander braced himself for the return of the famous Arles temper. But instead, those full lips quirked, and he lifted an eyebrow. "And you didn't think to mention this?"

Smirking, Sander hugged his knees to his chest. "You didn't ask."

"Anything else you might have forgotten to mention?" Tarik's tone held a buried laugh.

"Um... there's toothpaste and spare toothbrushes in the medicine locker?"

The laugh escaped, and from the expression on Tarik's face, he was just as startled by it as Sander. "At this point, I wouldn't be surprised if she had a hot tub and sauna."

Sander's stomach cramped again. "Not even a shower at this point. Not without water in the tank."

"Until tomorrow, then." This time, Tarik's tone was confident, bordering on smug.

Sander frowned up at him. "We don't know that. I probably won't be able to manipulate something as heavy as a bucket of water."

Tarik strolled toward *Askatasun*, patting Sander's shoulder on the way past. "I have complete confidence you'll do it brilliantly."

"At least one of us does," Sander muttered. He stared resolutely into the fire so he wouldn't be tempted to watch the shadows playing on Tarik's retreating form. When he caught the flare of the solar lanterns below deck out of the corner of his eye, he sighed at the missed opportunity and lay back on the blanket.

The stars arched overhead, not obscured by even a scrap of a cloud. But that could change overnight. Stranger things had happened than weather defying millennia of its normal pattern. *I'll unfurl the cockpit awning. Rig it to collect rainwater. Maybe a miracle will occur, we'll get a freak downpour, and I won't have to display my incompetence tomorrow.*

"I should be so lucky," he muttered, flinching when wood popped in the fire, sending a shower of sparks spiraling into the dark.

On the other hand, rescue might arrive with the dawn. Surely Sander's absence had been noticed by now. His marina crew was loyal and competent, and Luken relentlessly efficient. He wouldn't stop until he'd tracked Katalin down, even if it meant taking to the Tanzanian bush.

For that matter, surely someone would notice Tarik was missing. He was far more important and visible to North Abarra than Sander was to the South.

But does North Abarra have any way to track him? Sander could only hope Katalin finished hobnobbing with her elephants soon and sent her seagulls spies searching for him.

Speaking of seagulls... He raised himself onto his elbows, frowning. He'd been a little preoccupied today, but he didn't recall seeing a single pesky bird. *Better deploy the cockpit awning for their benefit, though.* Because they'd show up eventually—you couldn't escape the annoying buggers forever, and they weren't exactly discriminating about where they shit.

He slogged through the sand and climbed aboard, dawdling with the awning to make sure Tarik had time to finish getting ready for bed. Sander gulped. *He doesn't have any pajamas. I don't have any pajamas. Oh lord.*

He brushed the sand off his feet and crept through the companionway into the cabin. The curtain was drawn across the sea head and Sander could hear the unmistakable sound of toothbrushing. *Will he be naked when he walks out? Should I go back on deck until he's in the berth?*

The berth. He peered at it where it nestled innocently in the stern, its sea blue blankets and white linens as pristine as if *Askatasun* were resting at anchor off the coast of Monaco instead of listing, broken, on an inhospitable shore.

It had always seemed so roomy, but he'd never shared it with anyone before. When Katalin sailed with him, she'd always used the guest bunk that had been destroyed in the shipwreck. *Why didn't I opt for more sleeping space instead of more storage when I built this thing?*

Easy answer: He hadn't anticipated sharing with anybody except Katalin, and not very often at that. He'd built *Askatasun* fully expecting to be as alone on the sea as he was on land.

The curtain *swooshed* and Tarik strolled out, tipping the last of the water from his pouch into his mouth and swishing it about. He was still wearing his shorts, although he'd lost the shirt. Sander wasn't certain whether to be relieved or disappointed over either situation. After Tarik swallowed—*God, his throat*—he tilted his head and peered past Sander at the berth. "Left or right? Or should I say port or starboard, seeing as we're onboard ship here?"

Sander blinked, mesmerized by the curve of Tarik's neck. "I'm sorry. What?"

"Which side of the bed do you sleep on?"

"Oh. Um, the middle, actually."

Tarik lifted an eyebrow. "That won't fly this time. But since you're planning to get up to tend the fire, I'll take the inside." He ran a hand over his face, massaging his temples with his long, elegant fingers.

"Is your headache worse? Do you need more painkillers?"

Tarik's smile was wry as he eased past Sander to get to the berth. "My head is actually quite good. Besides, I avoid painkillers when I can. They only mask the pain."

"Yes, Tarik." Sander couldn't keep the snark out of his tone. "That's the whole point."

Tarik chuckled. "That's exactly what my cousin always says. Well, good night, Sander." And he shucked his shorts down his legs without the least hesitation before climbing under the covers and scooting across to lie on his side facing the hull. Naked.

Slack-jawed and dry-mouthed, Sander leaned against the bulkhead to keep from sliding onto the cabin sole. "G-good night," he croaked. He stumbled to the head to get himself ready—a process made difficult by a cock with an entirely different agenda, one involving Tarik's smooth brown skin and full lips.

When he finally emerged to douse the solar lanterns and secure the hatch, he still felt off balance. But that wasn't just his fevered imagination—he *was* off balance. Because *Askatasun* was listing to starboard, a ten-degree tilt to her decks. *And to her berth.*

And when roundish things like bodies lay on a tilted surface, they tended to roll. If Sander wasn't careful, he'd be plastered against Tarik's naked body by midnight.

"Not. Happening," he murmured through clenched teeth. He took off his windbreaker and pants, but left his boxer briefs on. *Like those are going to help.* He eased himself onto the mattress and curled on his side facing away from Tarik, as close to the edge as he could manage.

He fully expected to lie there, frozen in place, all night long. But whether it was the exertion of the day or the lulling lap of waves on the shore, before he knew it, he was blinking awake to find dawn brightening the port lights— and Tarik spooned along his back, one arm flung across Sander's chest and his cock nestled against Sander's ass.

Sander narrowly avoided a shriek—although he did gasp, making Tarik murmur something and shift closer.

Okay, clearly he's still asleep. I can't take this personally. Not Tarik's morning wood cradled in Sander's crease. Not Tarik's chest hair rough against Sander's back. Not Tarik's breath, warm against Sander's neck. *Not personal.*

His own cock wasn't buying it, of course.

He eased out from under Tarik's arm and off the edge of the bed. Good lord, if Sander had slept through the night, the signal fire could be out. His stomach jolted, but before panic could thrust him out on deck, he looked down at Tarik, his black curls fanned on the pillow, his dark skin such a lovely contrast against the white linens. In sleep, his face calm and at peace, he was beautiful. A beauty without the hard edges of angry Tarik or snarky Tarik.

A beauty I could love.

Sander grabbed a towel and fled above deck before he could do something stupid like stroke Tarik's hair or kiss his forehead.

The fire had indeed burned down, although embers still smoldered under a dusting of ash. Using the stack of driftwood Tarik cut yesterday, Sander built it up again. Then he stripped off his briefs and waded into the sea, which was about the same temperature as the air. He wasn't fond of salt water residue on his skin, doubled now since he'd taken a dip last night to rid himself of the sweat of the day's exertions. But unless he was able to pull off a miracle today and fill that damn bucket with water, it was the best option he had.

When he waded out of the gentle surf, Tarik was standing in *Askatasun*'s cockpit, bare-chested, gazing down at him. Sander *eep*ed, covering his groin with his hands, but Tarik just laughed and tossed him his towel and another pair of faded board shorts from the locker stash. *Thank God I keep extras on board.*

"Shall we give this experiment a go first thing, or do you need one of those charming emergency rations to build up your strength first?"

Sander dried off, none too thoroughly in his hurry, and when he stepped into the shorts, the fabric clung to his still-damp skin. "Might as well get it over with. Once we've proved I'm incapable, I can fish for our breakfast." He arranged his towel over the transom to dry. "*That* I know I can do."

"Hey." Tarik leaped onto the sand, proving that he was also wearing shorts, thank God. "You can do this too." He scooped up the bucket and handed it to Sander. "So how about showing me this famous waterfall and getting down to it?"

Sander glanced sidelong at *Askatasun*. *Should I grab my windbreaker?* But making a special trip would call more attention to their bare chests. *I can handle it. It's just skin. Really lovely brown skin. And chest hair. And—* He shook his hands out and took a deep breath. "All right. Let's go."

Two hours and a considerably more dented bucket later, Sander was ready to admit defeat. "This is impossible."

"It's not." Tarik held out the bucket again. "You can already levitate the thing across the crevasse with no trouble. You just need to brace for the force of the water. Try aiming for the edge of the falls this time. Ease the bucket partway under. It won't fill as fast, but it'll be easier to control."

Sander snatched the bucket and huffed out a breath. "Fine. One more time. But if it doesn't work, I'm done."

"It'll work." Tarik gripped his shoulder. "Trust me."

"It's not you I need to trust," Sander muttered. But he faced the falls, anyway. Tarik didn't release his shoulder, and for some reason, that grounded Sander in a way that had been missing before. He took a deep, calming breath, feeling the magnetic force surrounding him. In the earth. In the air. *In me.*

And the water. Water was a force too, generating its own formidable power. *But it doesn't have to be an incompatible power. Not if I invite its cooperation.*

He set his jaw and released the bucket. It held steady in the air. *Because the air isn't empty. It's a part of the field. It supports me. Welcomes me. Works with me.* He flicked his fingers and while the bucket didn't exactly sail across the distance—that experiment had been the major cause of the new dents—it moved forward steadily, like *Askatasun* before a following sea.

"Steady. Steady." Tarik's grip tightened on his shoulder. "Nearly there. You've almost got it. Now just dip the rim of the bucket under the edge."

Sander jerked his chin in terse agreement. *Finesse. Not force.* He kept a firm... well... *hold* for no better word and tilted the bucket just enough to catch the outer spill of the falls. The impact nearly tore it out of his grip, but he caught it, and the bucket began to fill.

"That's it," Tarik murmured. "You're doing great. Just a little more. Don't need to overdo it the first time."

Good point. The bucket was only half full, but a half full bucket was half a bucket more than they had before. Sander curled his fingers, beckoning it to return.

And it did, with barely a wobble, traveling through the air to his waiting hands.

He stared down at it, hardly able to believe it. "I did it." He set the bucket at his feet because his hands started to shake. He stood up and faced Tarik. "I did it." His grin threatened to split his face. "I really did it."

Tarik's grin answered his own. "You really did. Just like I knew you could."

Sander whooped, grabbed Tarik in a bear hug, and jumped up and down. Tarik laughed, returning the hug and joining in the pogo effect until Sander's foot struck the bucket. Which made Sander laugh harder, because how ironic would it be to lose the thing now from something as stupid as kicking it into the chasm?

Tarik's hands flattened on Sander's bare back. *No shirts. Shit.* Their bouncing hug had the effect of rubbing certain other parts of their anatomy together as well—certain parts that were showing interest in a different sort of celebration.

Awkward.

He released Tarik and stepped back, wiping his hands on his shorts. "I've got a water testing kit on the boat so we can check for potability. The vandals didn't bother with that. They just smashed one keg of wine—"

Tarik closed his eyes and lifted his hand to his forehead, palm out, like the swooning heroine in a melodrama. "Please, Sander. Please tell me there's more wine."

Sander's grin morphed into a full, joyful laugh, because even though they were stuck on an island with no way of communicating with the outside world, they had water. Water he'd fetched himself with powers he'd never thought to control.

He picked up the bucket, relishing its weight as he swung it at his side. "*Askatasun* belongs to the owner of Roses Estate Vineyards. Of *course* there's more wine."

When Tarik climbed out of the companionway, toweling his hair dry, Sander was crouched by the blazing signal fire, tending a much smaller fire in the little cast iron grill at his feet, with a platter of neatly filleted fish on a tray behind him.

Grinning, Tarik hung his towel over the gunwale. "I can't believe you have a hibachi."

"It's small and convenient." Sander shrugged. "I can't have electrics or electronics on the boat for obvious reasons. The galley only has a single propane burner, so this works better when I'm not actually at sea." He glanced up at Tarik, the fire casting interesting shadows over his face. *That smile.* Tarik was glad his lower half was blocked by the gunwale. "Thanks for catching all the fish."

"Thanks for cleaning them. And thanks for hauling enough water for me to shower." He shivered theatrically.

"Although your solar water heater needs an upgrade. The water still had a definite bite to it."

Sander smirked. "Why do you think I let you go first?"

Tarik laughed and jumped down onto the sand. "So it didn't have anything to do with wanting to wait until you were done with all the fish guts?"

"Hey." Sander stood, lifting his chin in mock haughtiness. "I gut fish with the precision of a neurosurgeon." He glanced down at his hands. "But as a matter of fact, yes. I did want to wait."

"It's all yours. I'll monitor the grill. I think it may be small enough not to strain my limited barbecue skills."

"Thanks. It should be ready for the fish shortly."

But Sander didn't head for the boat. Instead, he wandered down near the shore, peering into the darkness.

Tarik strolled up next to him. "What are you looking for?"

"Nothing really." His mouth twisted ruefully. "Well, *nothing* is the problem. I left the fish guts along there, next to the rocks. But I haven't seen a single seagull show up to take advantage of the free food."

"Maybe they haven't noticed yet."

Sander shot him a skeptical glance. "If you put fish guts on the moon, seagulls would find it inside of an hour. They're world-class scavengers with a beady eye on the main chance. But they haven't shown any interest in us at all."

Tarik had the oddest urge to smooth the wrinkle between Sander's eyebrows, as if that could erase his worry. "So you *want* seagulls to find us? I thought they were kind of annoying."

"They are. They're loud and pushy and not exactly picky about where they shit. But they're also the worst gossips in the bird kingdom." He smiled wryly. "It's how my sister keeps track of me when I'm on a sail."

"Your sis— Ah. Anime."

Sander nodded. "She always accompanies me on this particular trip. But she's in Tanzania right now, on contract with the Conservancy on an elephant poaching case." His smile turned fond. "She can never resist elephants."

The light dawned, making Tarik feel even more like an asshole. "That's how you knew we'd only be here for a week. Because the birds would tell your sister where you were."

He nodded again. "Yes. I put out the bait because the sooner the gulls get the message, the sooner it'll get to Katalin. But if none of them show up…" He shrugged. "Oh well. They'll show up, eventually. Kat may be unable to resist elephants, but seagulls can never resist fish guts." He held up his hands, wrinkling his nose, which was too fucking cute for words. "Now I'm going to go shower, because I can still smell them on me."

"Take your time."

Sander rolled his eyes. "I don't think so. We don't have *that* much water."

"Yeah, but that's the thing." Tarik grinned, waggling his eyebrows. "You can always get more tomorrow."

Tarik counted it a win that Sander was chuckling as he climbed into the cockpit and disappeared into the companionway.

From somewhere in *Askatasun*'s many storage lockers, Sander had unearthed a sweatshirt worn soft from age, and Tarik had put it on, but the night wasn't that cold. He wandered back to the signal fire, the breeze ruffling his curls.

Next to the hibachi, Sander had spread out several blue tarps and topped them with blankets, although Tarik had no illusions that that would keep sand completely out of the picture. A couple of plates, several glasses, a pitcher of water, and some flatware were stacked next to—*score!*—a small keg with the Roses Estate stamp on its head. *Guess if you're going to get stranded on a deserted island, having a fully equipped sailboat along is the way to go.*

Tarik sat down on the blanket and leaned back on his hands, his legs stretched in front of him. His headache from the attack was gone. He couldn't remember the last time he'd been pain free, completely clear of the constant noise of other people's lives as delivered over the airwaves.

Yep, definitely need to invest in an uninhabited island of my own.

He glanced at *Askatasun*'s bulk, where below her decks, Sander was currently naked. Tarik's dick stirred in his shorts—*Sander's shorts*—and he remembered the feel of Sander's body against his in that unexpected hug on the cliff's edge.

Sander Fiala was *built*.

Wide chest, defined pectorals, meaty biceps that begged for Tarik's teeth. And those forearms. *Ungh.*

He drew his legs in, curling over his knees and ordering his dick to stand the fuck down. Because this *was* Sander Fiala. Duke of Roses. *Monster* of Roses. The man North Abarran nannies invoked to frighten their charges into behaving. Tarik's country had been on the brink of war with Sander's a dozen times or more in the last century—hell, in the last decade. How could he be lusting after his enemy?

My enemy wouldn't look out for me so diligently. My enemy wouldn't haul water all day to give me a chance to shower. My enemy wouldn't fight his own fears to keep me alive.

Which led to the inescapable conclusion that Sander wasn't his enemy.

"Shit," he muttered to his knees and recalcitrant dick. "Politics is fucking stupid."

"That's what Katalin says."

Tarik's head shot up. Sander was grinning at him from the deck, his wet hair slicked back against his head. Tarik grimaced. "Heard that, did you?"

"Sound carries by the water." He hung his towel next to Tarik's. "Just before our first meeting—"

Tarik groaned. "Please don't remind me of what an asshole I was then."

With a chuckle, Sander jumped onto the sand. "It was impressive."

Tarik groaned again and rolled over to faceplant on the blanket, the better to hide his erection when Sander settled down, cross-legged, on the blanket next to him.

"Katalin grouses that political animosity ought to be worked out on a sports field."

"With visits to the nearest pub first so all the diplomats can raise a pint together before negotiations? Or maybe stage one of those tailgate parties the Americans are so fond of?"

Sander snorted. "I'd pay good money to see the Minister of Powers waving one of those giant foam fingers and wearing a beer hat." He picked up a long glass tube that Tarik recognized as a wine thief and held it over the keg. "Shall I draw some wine for you? It's our Roses Red Special Reserve blend. I know a lot of people get agitated about serving red wine with fish, but—"

"They can go fuck themselves." Since his dick was behaving itself for the moment, Tarik scrambled over and grabbed an empty glass. "Gimme. That's one of your best. Although the first time I tasted it, I wanted to murder you."

Sander's eyes widened and his fingers fumbled with the silicon bung stopper. "Uh…"

"Only in a business sense. Not in a, you know, stabby *murdery* sense."

Sander smirked. "Let me guess. The 2014 Wine Internationale competition?"

"The very same. I'm surprised you keep this on the boat instead of selling it at auction. I for one would have paid a fortune for it, if only to figure out how you could come up with something that so far surpassed our Royal Velvet with the same grapes on virtually the same fields."

"This isn't the 2014 vintage. It's the pressing from two years ago. Katalin and I were supposed to sample it on this cruise and let the head winemaker know if it's ready to bottle." Sander inserted the thief into the bunghole and drew out a tube full of wine that glowed ruby red in the firelight. He released the liquid into Tarik's glass.

"Thank you." Tarik swirled it, admiring the wine's color and clarity. Then he held it to his nose and inhaled deeply. *Ah.* So much better when it wasn't mixed with water and soaking into Tarik's wool suit. He took a sip, letting the flavors of citrus, plum, and spice expand and deepen on his tongue. "Damn, that's good. It might be better than the 2014, and I wasn't sure anything could be."

Sander filled his own glass. "When I sail, I like to remember all the reasons my life is good. This is one of them."

Tarik took another sip, eyes fluttering closed. "You know," he said dreamily, "I finally decided that the difference between our wines and yours must lie in the aging barrels. I've been trying for years to pry the name of your vendor from anyone who might know." He cracked an eyelid and peered at the keg. "Maybe I'll sneak out of bed tonight and search for the cooper's badge on that one."

Sander's eyes glinted over the rim of his glass. "Good luck. It doesn't have one. And you'll never get the cooper's name from my staff."

"I wouldn't even try. I'm not *that* big an asshole. But I grill all my suppliers regularly, offering them a ten percent markup on the same barrels they sell to Roses Estate."

"Only ten percent?" Sander shook his head, clucking his tongue. "Not much of an incentive for an industrial spy."

Tarik smiled sheepishly. "I may have upped it to fifty. Or two hundred." He shrugged. "Still no takers."

Sander raised his wine in a toast. "Congratulations. Your suppliers are honest."

"You mean incorruptible. Which…" He tapped his bottom lip with the glass, pretending to consider. "… is a good thing. I *suppose*."

"No, I mean they're really honest. None of them sell to Roses Estate."

"Then where do the barrels come from? Space?" He took another sip. "Because I could actually believe that."

"Hardly." Sander chuckled, a self-deprecating sound. "They come from me."

"You?" When Sander's brows drew together at Tarik's disbelieving tone, Tarik wanted to kick himself. "I know what your power is now, and it's not shitting out oak barrels." He winced. "Which is a good thing because that sounds fucking painful."

Sander nudged Tarik's leg with his foot. "No, you ass. I build them. By hand. The same way I built that boat. That's pretty much how I spend most days. In the woodshop."

Tarik didn't think his jaw sagged, but even if it did, Sander wouldn't have seen it. He was too busy staring down into the depths of his glass, as if creating an aging barrel that produced wine like this, or a boat with lines sleeker than half the yachts in Monte Carlo Harbor, was somehow shameful.

He's not a monster. He's not my enemy. He was just a man. *A man who's done nothing since this misadventure began but try to take care of me—to take care of us both.* A man who was doing the best he could with what fate threw at him—which included a grumpy, headache-prone, stowaway dickhead duke who should know better than to jump to conclusions.

"I'm sorry."

CHAPTER EIGHT

At Tarik's soft apology, Sander glanced up from his wine. "For what?"

"For a lot of things. For being such a prick to you from pretty much the moment we met."

Sander tucked his legs to his chest and wrapped one arm around them, balancing his glass on his kneecap. "Are you always like that?"

Tarik huffed a laugh. "Well, yeah. But usually it's because people are idiots and I know they're idiots because I've been receiving their idiot communications for so long that my head is ready to explode." He sighed. "But I had no call to treat you that way. I've never heard a peep from you over the airwaves."

Sander raised his glass in a mock toast. "Now you know why. I may be the only man in Abarra—North or South— who communicates exclusively through hand-written letters." He scrunched up his face. "I've got an old manual Underwood typewriter gathering dust in my study, but I can't get ribbons for it anymore. And to be honest, I really prefer using my grandfather's fountain pen."

Discussing deep feelings with the Duke of Arse? I really need more wine to have this conversation. But maybe drinking more on an empty stomach was stupid. He set his glass aside and transferred the fish to the hibachi, topping them with a few sprigs of the wild rosemary he'd found rioting on the hillside.

When he turned back, Tarik was regarding him steadily with those midnight-dark eyes. "Everyone treats you that way, don't they? Even if they don't do it to your face. They approach you with a set of expectations and don't bother to give you the chance to refute them."

The muscles in Sander's back tensed and his shoulders rose toward his ears. "They've got good reason."

Tarik's gaze didn't waver. "No. I don't think they do."

Definitely need more wine. Sander brandished the wine thief. "Top up?"

"I'm good, thanks." Tarik edged closer and placed a gentle hand on Sander's forearm. "Sander. Tell me what really happened. Tell me about that day."

"You mean the Disaster?"

"No. I mean the *accident.*"

Sander stared down at Tarik's brown hand, so gentle on his skin. His palm wasn't rough like Sander's, although his fingernails showed the effects of their recent manual labor. He sucked in a shaky breath. *Do I want to talk about this? I never talk about this. I never think about this if I can help it.*

"I need to turn the fish," he croaked.

Tarik nodded, squeezing Sander's arm gently before releasing it. "All right."

As Sander fumbled with the spatula, trying and failing to flip the fillets without breaking them, he kept glancing at that spot on his arm where the ghost of Tarik's touch lingered. *I should tell him the truth. So he'll know how dangerous I really am. So he'll know to keep his distance.*

The memory of Tarik's body, warm against his in the berth, resurfaced. *I don't want him to keep his distance.* But that was exactly the reason why he should. Sander's big, bluff father hadn't kept his distance, so certain he could find a way to help where the Ministry had failed, and had paid the price.

I can't do that to another person. I can't do that to Tarik.

He glanced sidelong at Tarik to find him gazing pensively into the signal fire, his face clear of any trace of the disgust and hostility of their early acquaintance. Would the truth bring it back? *If so, can I bear it?*

But who else had ever asked him to explain? To give his side of the story of that horrible day? Even Katalin and his mother avoided the subject, either out of their own grief or out of consideration for Sander's feelings.

And as for the officials at the Ministry of Powers, they'd never ventured into the same room, tossing their sharp questions over the PA system and sending a trembling technician in to restrain and sedate him. They'd bombarded him with test after test, always from behind fortifications that rivaled a nuclear bunker. Sander had only been a teenager, but he wasn't stupid. He knew what they wanted —to either lock his powers down so he couldn't threaten them or else weaponize it—weaponize *him*—to use against their enemies. *Enemies like Tarik.*

Would revealing the truth about his powers be an act of treason? Could Tarik, as a high-ranking North Abarran Royal, somehow use it against Sander's Queen and country?

If the Ministry couldn't find a way to use it, I doubt Tarik can. And as Sander scooped the fish onto their plates, he discovered that didn't care. *No. Not that I don't care. I don't believe he* would.

He offered Tarik a serving. "I'm afraid the poor fish kind of fell apart." He smiled wryly. "Apparently I'm better at gutting them than grilling them."

Tarik accepted the plate gravely. "I'm not that fussy about presentation. Although do you suppose we should sprinkle some of those emergency rations on top? They're the closest thing we've got to a lemon wedge."

Sander snorted a laugh. "I think I'll pass." He refilled their wine and settled, cross-legged, to eat his dinner. He wasn't sure if it was the contrast with the emergency rations, or that *Askatasun's* galley held enough staples to season it properly, but it wasn't bad.

Tarik groaned and Sander dropped his fork with a clatter. "Are you okay? Is it a bone? Do you—"

"This has got to be," Tarik murmured, his eyes at half-mast, "the best thing I've ever tasted."

This time Sander's laugh was more heartfelt. "That's only because you're comparing it to lemon-flavored emergency rations."

"Absolutely not. The best thing. Hands down." He shot Sander a thumbs-up.

"I'm not sure how seriously to take a review from somebody who doesn't know up from down," Sander said dryly, but returned to his own meal with a smile. It gradually faded though, and when he was reduced to toying with a sprig of singed rosemary, he couldn't delay any longer.

Sander set his plate aside and took a deep breath. "By the time I turned fifteen, everyone knew that getting electronics or any machine with solid-state circuits near me was a mistake. My family lived in Castle Abarra then. It was before Aunt Maialen ascended the throne, but my mother was already part of her diplomatic corps. My father was on Grandfather's cabinet. Minister of Industry."

Tarik regarded him somberly. "His power moniker was Mechanico, wasn't it? I remember hearing about the work he did with retrofitting factories."

"Yes." Sander's lips trembled at the memory of his father, who, despite anything his mother said, could never believe he wasn't invincible. "It was his dream to bring the country's infrastructure into the modern age, so he spent a lot of time away from the Castle. It was just his bad luck that he was there that day."

"What happened?"

The gentleness in Tarik's tone threatened to close Sander's throat. He took a sip of wine. "I... I went off."

"Went off?"

Sander nodded, giving silent thanks that he stocked *Askatasun* with sturdier glassware than Luken insisted for the Manor. Otherwise, this one would have shattered in his white-knuckled grip. "My father had called to me from his office. I never went in there—he didn't have any sophisticated equipment in there, but he had samples of the machinery he'd already replaced in some of the factories. He always said there was no danger, but I didn't want to take the chance. I hated the idea of accidentally destroying anything he was working on. But that day, he— I—" Sander clenched his eyes shut and bowed his head, inhaling in short gasps.

"Sander." Tarik's hand settled on the back of Sander's neck. "You don't have to do this."

But the warmth of Tarik's palm spread a balm over Sander's raw nerves. "I do," he croaked. He took a deep, shuddery breath. "I do."

"Then I'm honored to listen." Tarik started to release his grip, but Sander laid his palm over it.

"Don't let go. Please. Your touch... helps."

"All right." Tarik's thumb stroked gently along Sander's nape. "Whatever you need."

"He laughed when I stopped in the sitting room." Sander opened his eyes but kept his gaze focused on Tarik's knee. He couldn't look him in the face. Not now. "Told me I was being foolish and gestured for me to join him. He... he had an experiment he wanted to try. A new kind of shield that he thought might help my condition. He said... he said, 'I can't very well test it with you standing halfway to Dulibre, Sander. Come here.' So I did."

"You went into his office."

"Not all the way." Sander's gaze flew to Tarik, willing him to understand. "I stopped with my hand on the doorframe. He was holding something in his hand. I don't even know what it was. I didn't see it clearly. And then suddenly, something *built* in me—my chest, my head, my hands. I couldn't see anything and my muscles all seized. My fingers dug into the doorframe so deep I had splinters the size of toothpicks under my nails. But then it just... burst. Out of me. At everything around me. At him."

"Shit," Tarik muttered, his thumb pausing in its stroke for only an instant.

"I passed out. When I came to, I was in the Castle dungeon."

"What the fuck?" Tarik shouted. He let go of Sander to roll to his knees, eyes blazing. "They locked you in a fucking *dungeon*?"

"We call it the dungeon, but it's really a series of nicely equipped holding cells, some of them for medical evaluation." Sander managed a weak smile. "And they had cause, Tarik. Whatever had happened, whatever... force I'd channeled, I brought down the ceiling in my father's office, destroyed the wiring in half the Castle, and fried, melted, or exploded every piece of equipment plugged into an outlet. They'd dug me out from under a pile of debris." He swallowed and looked away. "It took them longer to reach my father because the structural integrity of the Castle had been damaged. He wasn't the only casualty. There were others." *Sixteen*. Sander still named each one before he was able to sleep every night. "And a lot of injuries."

Tarik's mouth was set in a grim line, his jaw tight. *I knew it. Disgust. Horror. Revulsion.* Sander couldn't expect any less, although he'd hoped—

"Didn't those idiots at least *try* to figure out why? Help you learn how to control it? Identify it, for fuck's sake?"

Sander blinked. *He's not angry at me?* "There have been rogue powers before. You should know better than anybody."

Tarik winced. "I suppose you're referring to Louis IV."

Sander smiled crookedly. "Well, South Abarran primary schools trot out tales of the Mad King as proof of the degeneracy of North Abarra at the earliest opportunity. I think I heard it first in kindergarten. Or maybe the nursery."

"Trust me, they do the same thing in North Abarra. Primary *and* secondary. Universities. Hell, at every corner pub, especially on Bonfire Night when we can burn the fucker in effigy." Tarik glared into the flames. "Stupid ancestors and their inbreeding. Thank God they passed the consanguinity laws." He looked up, his expression still fierce. "But that was centuries ago. And you were only fifteen, so why the fuck didn't somebody *help* you?"

Sander shrugged. "The last thing anyone wanted to do was traumatize me more. I'd killed my father and sixteen others. Injured dozens more, including Grandfather. The last thing *I* wanted to do was talk about it. So they sent me out into the country, to a cottage on our estate that..." Sander swallowed against the lump in his throat. "... that Father hadn't gotten around to upgrading yet." He managed a shaky smile. "Very rustic. Very bucolic. Very... isolated."

"Very fucking medieval. For fuck's sake, you were a kid who'd just lost his father, and they sent you into solitary confinement."

Sander traced a line in the blanket with one finger. "I wasn't alone. Luken, my valet, was with me. My mother came to visit when she could. So did my sister and one of my cousins."

"Zorion?"

Sander shook his head. "No. It was Otho, the one who's royal courier now. Grandfather wouldn't, um, risk Zo. Or Aunt Maialen. In case I went off again."

"Protecting the succession," Tarik growled. "I get it. But I don't have to like it."

A kernel of warmth bloomed in Sander's belly. "You almost sound like you care."

Tarik's dark eyes met his and Sander's mouth went dry at the heat he read there, heat that had nothing to do with the flames crackling in the driftwood and sad wreckage of his boat.

Sander looked away, unready to act on that heat, afraid it would consume him, consume them both. "Anyway, that's where I built my first barrel. I still use it as my workshop." He took a gulp of wine, a crime against this vintage. "So now you know. I'm a rogue. An uncontrolled power." He tipped the rest of the wine into his mouth. "A monster."

"You're not," Tarik said fiercely. "You're the furthest thing from a monster I've ever met. Fuck, *I'm* more a monster than you are."

A smile ambushed Sander's lips. "There are any number of people who'd agree with that. But most of them are either discredited or in prison because you uncovered their secrets."

Tarik's white teeth gleamed in the firelight. "I can't argue with that. And I can't say I'm sorry either. They all deserved it. But you, Sander?" Tarik reached up and slowly traced Sander's cheek with one gentle finger. "You don't deserve any of it."

Sander was frozen under that touch, Tarik's fingertip like an ember on his skin, igniting something in his chest, in his belly, in his—*God*—in his groin. Nobody had ever made him feel like this. Not that he'd had much opportunity for experimentation, given his isolation.

There'd been an engineer who'd helped him with a waterwheel and was very good with his, er, hands. A toolmaker who'd crafted a custom spokeshave for him and delivered it personally with a blow job bonus. But other than that? Sander had no experience with how this worked. Those other men had been attractive enough, willing enough—or maybe they were just reckless enough to dare the touch of the Monster of Roses.

But Tarik was his enemy. Wasn't he? Parliament would certainly say so. Parliament would likely brand Sander a traitor for not tossing Tarik into the sea with the anchor chain wrapped around his neck, considering how many of their former members had been discredited by Wavelength's testimony.

But Parliament wasn't here. Nobody was here. Not even the gossipy seagulls were here to carry tales to his sister. Only Tarik. *And me.*

Sander knew—in the part of his brain that wasn't totally focused on the way Tarik's hand was cupping his jaw—that nothing could come of this. They were on opposite sides of so many tables. But right here? Right now? It was like a hookup in the world's most exclusive open-air club. *What happens on the island stays on the island.*

So Sander raised a shaking hand and as he'd been aching to do since he'd first seen Tarik, carded his fingers through Tarik's curls. They were just as soft, just as deliciously springy, as Sander had imagined they'd be. And when Tarik closed his eyes and groaned? *God.* Sander's cock hardened so fast he was dizzy.

"Fuck, that feels good," Tarik murmured.

"Your hair is beautiful." All the blood that wasn't in Sander's cock rushed up his throat. "I mean…" *Oh screw it.* "*You're* beautiful."

Tarik's eyes opened, but remained heavy-lidded. *Bedroom eyes.* "I'm glad you think so. Most people never make it past the perpetual scowl."

Sander ran his thumb over Tarik's high, smooth forehead. "You're not scowling now."

Tarik's lips curved in a wicked smile. "Maybe because this is the first time since my power manifested that I don't have a headache. Or maybe..." His voice lowered to a suggestive purr. "... because an incredibly sexy man is inches away from me and petting me like he's got a very interesting agenda." His hand traced Sander's collarbone. "Do you? Have an agenda?"

"M-maybe?" Nobody had ever called him sexy before, and since his voice had risen to a near squeak, probably nobody ever would again. But he took his courage in his hands and outlined Tarik's full lower lip. "It has to do with your lips."

Tarik hummed, the sound vibrating in Sander's fingers. "My lips. Tell me more."

Sander nodded and the lips in question parted in a grin. "Your lips. And, um, mine."

"Now that..." Tarik edged closer until his body heat, even muffled by Sander's old Roses Estate sweatshirt, nearly scorched Sander's arm. "... is an agenda I fully approve." He angled his head. "Allow me to assist."

And then he pressed his soft, full, sinfully plush lips to Sander's. For an instant, Sander's brain fried like one of the countless cell phones that had fallen victim to him in the past seventeen years. Before he could get fully with the program and hold up his part of the kiss, Tarik drew back, concern knotting his forehead.

"Did I overstep? I'm sorry. I thought—"

"No!" Sander rolled to his knees, the better to cradle Tarik's face in his hands. "This is totally on the agenda. In fact, the agenda has *pages* devoted to this. But, well, I'm not that experienced." He shrugged. "Not many people want to date a monster."

Tarik's eyes narrowed for an instant. "I think I've mentioned before—people are idiots. But..." His wicked smile bloomed again. "I'm more than happy to take advantage of their lack of intelligence and add a training module to our agenda. Because Sander? I *do* have experience."

"A... a lot?"

"Enough. And I'm more than happy to share that experience with you."

So Tarik might have been exaggerating about his experience. He'd had hook-ups now and then before Bastien started his campaign to find Tarik a politically expedient soul mate, but they'd barely scratched an itch he couldn't even describe. Physical release, maybe, but nothing that made him want to repeat the experience with any of his partners, and no kissing to speak of. *Mouths were usually otherwise engaged.*

Later, after the courtship parties commenced, he'd kissed because it was expected, not from any true desire. It had been... pleasant. Sometimes. Other times, not so much, although he'd always secretly hoped that it could be more.

Well, now he knew. It could definitely be more. It could be *everything*, because nothing, *nothing* in any of those encounters had prepared him for kissing Sander. Fuck, their lips had barely touched. Seconds, if that. But the zing that had traveled down Tarik's spine had been enough for his dick to nearly punch through his shorts.

Now I get it. He was so onboard with the snogging agenda. *We can explore together, learn together.* Tarik had no worries that he'd lose interest halfway as he'd done in the past. That brief touch of Sander's lips? The stroke of

Sander's fingers through his curls? Tarik was still tingling from his toes to the ends of every hair on his head. *Talk about animal magnetism. What would his hand on my dick feel like?*

He buried a snort, because God forbid Sander think Tarik was mocking him. But Tarik suspected Sander could manhandle him as expertly as he'd learn to manipulate the water bucket. *If I'm lucky.*

Suddenly, it was desperately important for Sander to understand how much he was worth. So Tarik got his knees under him and faced Sander head on, chest to chest. "You are, without a doubt, the most beautiful man I've—"

"Don't say that. I know I'm all right, but—"

"—ever been stranded on a deserted island with."

Sander barked a laugh. "Now that, I'll accept."

"Then accept this too." Tarik laced his fingers behind Sander's neck, brushing his thumbs along Sander's throat. "I don't think I've ever desired anyone as much as I desire you. But despite what my past behavior might suggest, I'm fully aware that not everything is about me. You have a choice here too, Sander. Maybe the only one. So tell me. Do you want this? Do you want me?"

Sander's Adam's apple moved under Tarik's fingers as he swallowed. "More than I've ever wanted anything in my life."

"Thank fuck for that," Tarik breathed.

No matter how much he ached for Sander's mouth, he didn't dive for the man because Sander deserved so much more. He deserved attention and tenderness and consideration—something he'd obviously never gotten from most of the people in his life. So Tarik angled Sander's head just so. Tilted his own in the opposite direction. Brought them together for a touch, a taste, a promise.

Like coming home.

Sander's lips were warm and soft against Tarik's, igniting that same inner lightning as their first kiss, and when Tarik teased the seam with his tongue, Sander groaned low in his throat and let Tarik in. He tasted of wine and rosemary, and Tarik moaned as he stroked inside that welcoming heat. Still careful. Still gentle, because this was new to Sander and wasn't all that familiar to Tarik either.

But Sander was a damn quick study, because he met Tarik's strokes with his own, each one bolder, more assured, more masterful than the last. When Tarik suckled on his tongue, Sander *growled* and pulled away with a gasp.

"Come back," Tarik whimpered.

Sander stared at him, panting, his pupils blown wide and reflecting the firelight. *Fuck, he's having second thoughts. This was too much. Too soon. Too—*

But then Sander lunged at Tarik, sending them sprawling onto the blanket with Sander on top.

Tarik gazed up at him, so wild and beautiful. "You're not finally giving in to your first impulse to kick my ass, I hope."

Sander shook his head, a sly smile dawning as he shifted his hips to align their dicks. "Not *kick* it. Although it may figure on the agenda in some fashion."

"Oho." Tarik grinned. "This agenda gets more interesting all the time. I suggest we get back to it."

Sander gently brushed Tarik's hair off his forehead, concern flickering across his face. "Tarik. I hope you know my agenda isn't *generic*. It's *customized*."

"All the best agendas are." Tarik slipped his hands under Sander's windbreaker and trailed his fingers across the smooth skin.

"They are." Sander nodded solemnly. "And this really is all about you."

"That's where you're wrong." Tarik kissed Sander's chin, blond stubble grazing his lips. "It's all about *us*."

Sander's eyes fluttered closed as he growled again. And then *he* dove for Tarik, their kisses turning almost feral as they ate at each other's mouths.

I need more. I need skin.

So as much as he hated to break the connection, Tarik tore himself away and rolled them over. Their feet collided with something in a *clash* and *clatter*.

Sander chuckled breathlessly. "There goes the remains of dinner."

"As long as we don't kick over the wine and my feet aren't roasting on the hibachi, I don't care. Do you?"

In reply, Sander laced his fingers in Tarik's hair and pulled him down into another searing kiss. Two. Ten. Twenty? Fuck, Tarik lost count and who needed to keep score, anyway? All that mattered was Sander's mouth, Sander's moans, Sander's heat.

Sander.

"This," Sander murmured between one kiss and the next, "will never work." *Kiss. Moan. Kiss some more.* "Our countries are bitter"—*kiss*—"enemies."

Tarik stopped long enough to gaze into Sander's eyes. "The only people on this particular country are the two of us." He waggled his eyebrows. "You want to fight?"

Sander's fingers dipped below the waistband of Tarik's shorts. "God, no."

"Good." Tarik planted one more kiss on Sander's mouth, then levered himself up so he could strip off his borrowed sweatshirt and unzip Sander's windbreaker. As Tarik had hoped, Sander had no shirt on underneath. *Because he loaned his only T-shirt to me. To protect me from the sun. To take care of me.*

The thought made Tarik's dick throb as much as the sight of Sander's naked chest. He wanted to feel that chest against his, skin to skin, heart to heart, but first...

He leaned down and nuzzled between Sander's pecs, reveling in the scent—salt and ozone, like a storm at sea. He trailed kisses over to one nipple, suckling on it as it hardened under his tongue. He bit it gently and was rewarded with Sander's moan.

By now, Sander's hands were splayed over Tarik's ass cheeks, the calluses on his palms a tender abrasion. "God. *Tarik*."

"I've changed my mind."

Sander tensed. "About what?"

Tarik raised his head and grinned down at him. "The fish isn't the best thing I've ever tasted." Tarik licked a path upward to nibble on Sander's collarbone. *"You're* the best thing I've ever tasted."

Sander squirmed as Tarik dropped open-mouthed kisses up his throat. When Tarik sucked on the tender skin below his ear, Sander uttered a hoarse shout and withdrew his hands from Tarik's shorts—*damn it*—to flail about at his sides until he bunched the blanket in his fists, sending sand pattering around them.

"Gah! Tarik!" Sander gasped. "That… That…"

"That's going to leave a mark." Tarik kissed the spot softly, gentling it with his tongue. "Do you mind?" Sander shook his head wildly. "Excellent." Tarik carded his fingers through the silk of Sander's hair. "I'd like to see more of you. *All* of you. If you don't mind."

"As long as you return the favor." His eyes glinted with mischief. "Although I've already had a sneak preview."

Tarik blinked. "You… Oh. The first morning when I was rinsing out my suit." *Fuck, was that only yesterday? How did this happen so fast?* Tarik didn't stop to ask himself exactly what "this" was, because he had better things to think about —the avid expression on Sander's face, for one.

"Very impressive. But..." He brushed his fingers over Tarik's erection. "I think it might be even more impressive now."

Tarik bit his lip, because if Sander added any friction at all, Tarik would erupt in his pants. So he eased himself away, covering his retreat by scooting down to hover over Sander's stomach. He tucked his fingers under Sander's waistband, offering a brief prayer of thanks for drawstrings and elastic. "May I?"

Sander nodded, heat flaring in his eyes, fingers clenched in the blankets as he lifted his hips. Tarik eased the shorts down, inch by tantalizing inch, revealing the deep V of Sander's Adonis belt, torturing himself, torturing them both. When Sander's dick popped free—long, thick, and cut, veins standing out against the rosy skin—Tarik's jaw dropped.

"Fuck. Now I know why they call you the Monster."

Sander gave a strangled laugh. "Stuff it, Arles."

"Believe me, I'd like to," Tarik said admiringly. *I can't resist.* He swirled his tongue across the head, capturing a bead of salty pre-come as Sander fell back with a groan. "Please tell me you didn't forget to stock your boat with lube and condoms."

"Lube, yes. Condoms, no." Sander's face was flushed adorably in the dancing firelight. "I don't... entertain much."

Good. Did it make Tarik an asshole that he was glad Sander hadn't shared this level of intimacy with anyone else? Maybe. *But then, I know I'm an asshole.* And this time, he'd own it without a single qualm.

He tugged Sander's shorts back up, settling them at his waist with a last stroke to his dick. Then he stood and offered Sander a hand. "As I recall, there's a very comfortable bunk aboard *Askatasun*, with a notable absence of sand and discarded cutlery. What do you say we take it for a spin?"

CHAPTER NINE

Sander fidgeted next to the berth, the lube from the medicine locker in his hand, his breath never seeming to make it to the bottom of his lungs.

This is happening. I'm doing this. We're *doing this.*

Tarik had insisted Sander use the head first, arguing that it was only fair since he'd had the first shower, but when Sander emerged, Tarik was nowhere in the cabin.

Before Sander could panic though, Tarik climbed through the hatch. "I brushed off as much as I could up top, and what I couldn't manage, your bucket took care of. No sand tonight." He winked. "Only Sander."

Sander chuckled weakly. "Believe it or not, I wasn't always called Sander. Katalin started it when I took up woodworking."

"So it's not just a nickname?"

"Nope. It's also what I do."

Tarik smirked. "Not all you can or will do tonight, though. Not if I have any say in the matter." He ducked behind the curtain, whistling.

Whistling? Isn't he nervous? I'm nervous. *I think I've verging on a panic attack.* Sander stumbled to the galley sink and pumped water into a tin cup, but gulping it down didn't ease his dry mouth. *What if I disappoint him? What if his temper gets the better of him? What if—*

Tarik stepped back through the curtain.

Naked.

There's not enough water in the world *to wet my throat now.*

But as Tarik prowled toward him, his cock—long and brown and glorious—slapping against his taut belly, Sander yearned for another way entirely to soothe his thirst.

His cock. My mouth. What would he taste like?

"Sander."

"Hmmm?"

"My eyes are up here."

Sander's gaze shot to Tarik's face. "Sorry," he croaked.

But Tarik just smiled, and Sander's heart stuttered in his chest. Because this smile wasn't smug or mocking or wicked. It was almost... fond. As if Tarik found Sander worthy of affection. *It's not his fault if I want more.*

He reached Sander in another two strides—*Askatasun* wasn't *that* big—and placed his elegant hands on Sander's bare shoulders. Sander got lost in the heat in those coffee-dark eyes. *Deeper than the sea. Darker than the night sky.*

"Are you planning to wear those shorts to bed?"

Sander blinked. "What?" He glanced down. "Oh. Right." He started to shove his shorts down, but Tarik grasped his wrists.

"Allow me."

He waited for Sander's nod, then dropped a kiss on Sander's lips, his shoulder, and one nipple. *Gah!* Then he tucked his thumbs under Sander's waistband and lowered himself to his knees, taking the shorts along with him.

"I'm going to lift your feet now, Sander, so lean on me." Tarik didn't move again until Sander braced his hands on those lovely wide shoulders. Then he lifted each of Sander's feet in turn, slipping the shorts free before flinging them across the cabin to land next to the berth. He looked up. "I'd like to suck you. May I?"

Is that a trick question? "Please." Sander's voice was nothing but a thread, but Tarik must have heard him, because in the next instant, his cock was engulfed in the most heavenly wet heat imaginable. "Tarik," he breathed.

Then Sander's imagination was challenged once more because Tarik begin to suck, and *that* was the best thing imaginable—until he added a tight grip around the base, jacking Sander as he tongued the slit. Sander's eyes fluttered closed without his permission and he clutched Tarik's shoulders, willing himself not to thrust because... because... *There's a reason, but I can't remember right now.*

But Tarik pulled off with a pop. "I don't want you to come yet." He nuzzled Sander's balls. "I want you to fuck my crease."

Mind. Blown. Again. "You what? I what?"

Tarik rose gracefully to his feet and framed Sander's face with both hands. "Don't worry." He kissed Sander, soft and slow, tongue flirting with Sander's. "I'll show you what to do. You've got the lube?" Sander nodded, still unable to speak. "Better grab one of those super fluffy towels to throw over the bed though." He winked again. "As wonderful as *Askatasun* is, I don't think she runs to housekeeping and turndown service."

"Right. Towel. Got it."

Sander managed to fumble a towel out of the locker in the bow, grateful for Katalin's extra linens obsession. When he stumbled back to the stern, Tarik was standing next to the berth, the tube of lube in his hand. Sander flung the blankets aside haphazardly. As soon as he'd laid the towel across the mattress, Tarik brushed by him, touching more skin than Sander was aware he possessed, and sat on the edge of the bed.

He crooked a finger. "Come closer." As if there were a tow line attached to that finger, Sander scooted forward. Tarik squirted a dollop of lube onto one palm, warming it with the other. He looked up, and Sander got lost in his gaze again, squeaking when Tarik's slick hands closed around his cock.

"That feels... Mmmm." Sander couldn't keep himself from thrusting this time, the lube easing the way through Tarik's tight grip.

"That's right, darling. Just like that."

Darling? Does he know he said that? Does he mean it?

But then his grip tightened and coherent thought fled out the open port light.

"Now." Tarik dropped a kiss on Sander's belly. "I'm going to lie face down on the bed."

"Unnnhhh?" *His hands...*

"And you're going to take this incredible cock of yours and slide it along my crease."

"Unnnhhh?" *His voice...*

"And I'm going to squeeze my cheeks together, the better to feel you, until you come all over my back and I come all over that towel." He nipped Sander's hip, breaking him out of his trance. "Can you slip that into your famous agenda?"

Sander nodded wildly, and as soon as Tarik was prone, all lovely brown skin and smooth muscle, Sander knelt on the bed, his knees bracketing Tarik's thighs. He ran his hands over Tarik's back, from his shoulder blades to the cleft of his ass.

The Duke of Arse indeed.

"So beautiful," he murmured, and eased his slippery cock along Tarik's crease. Tarik canted his hips a bit to change the angle. *Am I sliding over his taint? His hole?* Sander couldn't tell, since those parts were hidden, but he trusted Tarik to know what felt good. As he thrust, harder and faster, mesmerized by the way Tarik's brown skin contrasted with his own ruddy cock, he realized that he was almost howling, and Tarik wasn't any quieter.

Who cares? Nobody's around to hear us. Not even the bloody seagulls.

Tarik snaked his hand under him, and from the way his elbow was moving, he was jacking himself in time with Sander's thrusts. That sight, coupled with the way Tarik clenched his cheeks around Sander's cock—*as he said he would*—sparked something in Sander's balls that arrowed straight up his spine. He clenched his jaw around a groan as he shot, his come painting Tarik's back in creamy loops.

An instant later, Tarik shouted, his grip on Sander's cock tightening as his muscles tensed. His hips jerked once, twice, three times, and he subsided onto the mattress with a sigh.

Sander rolled to the side, careful not to crush Tarik's arm. Tarik's eyes were closed, and his smile was positively beatific. His eyelashes fluttered, and if Sander had thought the smile was heavenly before... *Good lord.*

"Thank you," Tarik murmured. "That was... Well, I'd tell you what it was, but apparently no words remain in my brain."

A chuckle caught Sander by surprise. Where was the doubt, the anxiety, the melancholy that had followed his other encounters? *I need to stop expecting Tarik to be like anybody else.* "I'll be right back."

Unable to blame the deck tilt on his unsteadiness—at least not entirely—he padded to the bow to collect another towel and a washcloth. He cleaned himself up in the head before returning to the berth to gently mop his own spend off Tarik's back—which amazingly enough, made Tarik giggle.

"If you'll move over, I'll get rid of the, er, used towel."

"That's what I like. A man who takes charge of the wet spot."

They got settled again, tucked under the blankets, and to Sander's surprise, Tarik nestled against him, head on Sander's chest.

Tarik sighed happily. "Thank goodness we didn't waste our time in this berth tonight."

"You kind of didn't last night either."

Tarik jerked away, horror dawning in his eyes. "Fuck, I didn't *molest* you, did I? Because I never meant—"

"Shhh." Sander laid a finger over Tarik's mouth. "It was just a cuddle. You were asleep." He traced the bow of Tarik's top lip. "To be honest, it was lovely. Nobody's ever done that with me before." He pulled Tarik against him again. "Poor *Askatasun* has never seen this much action."

"Askatasun." Tarik hummed low in his throat, a considering sound. "It's a Basque word, isn't it?"

Sander nodded, Tarik's curls soft against his throat. "A lot of our family names are, too. Grandfather insisted. He wanted our Basque heritage to endure. Although when Great-Aunt Josune married an Italian count, her branch veered more toward Roman names, which is why I have an uncle named Gaius and cousins named Cassian, Felix, and Otho."

Tarik rose on one elbow, propping his chin on his fist. "What does it mean? Askatasun?"

Sander smiled up at him, twining one dark curl around his finger. "Freedom."

"Freedom," Tarik murmured, his gaze unfocused. "I can see that. None of the judgmental bullshit can follow you when you're sailing."

"That's right." Sander turned his head and kissed Tarik's wrist. "The only time I feel free is when I'm at her helm." *Until now.*

A furrow appeared between Tarik's eyebrows. "But it's lonely too, isn't it? Single-handed sailing?"

"It can be. But I've never minded." *Until now.* Sander swallowed convulsively. He suspected that when next he put out to sea, he'd be looking constantly over his shoulder, searching for someone who would never be there again. Listening for Tarik's step on the deck, his voice in the cabin, his laugh on the wind.

But for now, Tarik was here, in Sander's berth. *Naked.* And judging by the heat and weight of Tarik's cock at Sander's thigh, ready for another round.

So Sander drew Tarik down into a kiss, rolling his own hips to slide his cock against Tarik's, and sent a jolt of heat singing along his veins.

Worries can bloody well wait.

Tarik came awake the next morning with his raging erection nestled snugly in the cleft of Sander's ass.

He took a moment to savor the peace—the dawn glow brightening the port lights, the scent of Sander's skin, the sound of the waves lapping on the shore.

Tarik didn't ordinarily lounge in bed in the morning. As soon as he woke, he was up and tackling the first tasks of the day. Of course, ordinarily his headache wouldn't let him go back to sleep, and nowadays when everybody slept with their fucking cell phones, the airwaves were never silent.

Except now. Except here.

How long had it been since he'd *wanted* to stay in bed? How long had it been since he'd had a *reason* to stay in bed? A reason like the incredibly sexy duke currently wrapped in his arms, skin warm against Tarik's chest, ass cradling Tarik's cock so perfectly.

"Mmmm." He pressed a kiss between Sander's shoulder blades.

Sander's chuckle vibrated under Tarik's arm. "Good morning."

"Yes. It is." He nuzzled Sander's ridiculously perfect nape. He'd promised to fish again while Sander hauled more water, but the emergency rations weren't *that* bad. They could make do with them this morning in favor of another round of lovemaking.

Lovemaking? Seriously?

But the way they'd come together last night had fit that definition exactly. It had been tender. Caring. Meaningful. *Important.* Important in a way that made his assurances to Bastien that he'd be perfectly happy with an arranged political marriage into total fucking bullshit.

Because now that he knew Sander—and not just in the Biblical sense—Tarik couldn't imagine making do with anyone else. Because that's what any marriage that arose from one of Bastien's damn courtship parties would be now —making do.

But does he feel the same?

Well, one way to find out.

Tarik slid his hand down Sander's chest, over his taut stomach, following the trail of silky hair to the treasure of Sander's dick in its nest of springy curls. "What do you say we—"

Sander jerked away, scrambling out of Tarik's arms and almost taking a header out of the berth when his feet got tangled in the bedding. Tarik's heart took its own nosedive. *Guess I've got my answer.*

"Shit. Damn. Motherfu—" Sander wrestled with the sheets, ripping them away from his feet so he could stand up. He threw open a locker next to the berth and pulled out another pair of faded shorts.

"I'm sorry." Tarik rolled onto his back. "I should have asked first."

Sander gazed down at him, one foot in the shorts, a frown pleating his forehead. "What?"

"I shouldn't have assumed that you'd want to—"

"Oh, God, Tarik." He threaded his fingers through Tarik's curls and nearly bashed his head against the bulkhead when he leaned down to drop a quick kiss on Tarik's lips. "That's not it." He let go and finished putting on his shorts. "I hear an engine."

"What?" Tarik sat up so fast he *did* bash his head. "Fuck." *Just when my headache was gone.* Sander disappeared around the bulkhead and through the hatch as Tarik scrambled out of bed. He checked the locker. More shorts. Thank God he and Sander had the same approximate waist size. He pulled on a pair and headed up the companionway, still tightening the drawstring.

Damn, Sander's ears must be good, because Tarik was only just now registering the sound of a small aircraft engine. He shaded his eyes and spotted it, still a ways off but on a heading that should send it over the northern edge of their beach.

Sander was standing in *Askatasun*'s bow, the signal mirror from the emergency kit in his hand. "Tarik. Build up the fire, please." *Good point.* They'd turned in so early—*for reasons*—the blaze had burned low overnight.

"On it." Tarik jumped to the sand and rushed to their wood pile. He chucked the first driftwood chunks in before he realized that he needed to be more strategic about this. So he fed in enough kindling to get the blaze going and *then* chucked in more driftwood. By the time he'd gotten it established, flames leaping as high as his head, the plane had buzzed closer, the size of a sparrow rather than a dragonfly in the brightening sky.

Brightening sky. Would the glare of the rising sun prevent anyone from seeing their fire? The plane's trajectory wouldn't take them directly over the SOS. If the pilot happened to be looking southeast, they might be able to see the signals, but why would they look out the window directly into the rising sun?

I've got to do something else.

Tarik glanced around wildly and his gaze caught on those ridiculously fluffy white towels draped over the gunwale. He stumbled over and snatched both of them, then ran for the rocks, as close to the plane's flight path as he could get.

He flapped the towels over his head in a crazy dance. "Hey! Over here!" *Stupid. They can't hear me.* But that didn't stop him. He kept dancing and flapping and shouting, despite the burning in his arms, the cramps in his legs, the rawness in his throat, until the plane passed just north of the island, never veering from its course.

Tarik let his arms drop, chest heaving, as Sander appeared at his elbow, signal mirror still in his hand.

"I don't understand. They had to have to seen us. The fire, the mirror, the SOS, your towel semaphore. Why aren't they at least diverting for a fly-over?"

At the distress in Sander's voice, Tarik turned, ready to wrap him in a hug and tell him everything would be all right. *And that might not even be a lie.*

But then the shoe dropped, along with Tarik's jaw. "Fuck me sideways with a chainsaw. Lightbender."

Sander glanced at him, but didn't stop deploying the signal mirror. "What?"

"Not what. Who. Lightbender is a non-Abarran supo who can create persistent illusions that mask sight, sound, and smell." He snorted a humorless laugh. "She works for a special effects studio in London, but she's not above picking up a gig on the side with no questions asked."

Sander's brows drew together, his expression like thunder, and the mirror fell from his lax fingers onto the sand. "You mean we're cloaked? Invisible? Nobody can see us? Hear us? Even *smell* us?" His eyes widened. "Not even the seagulls?"

"That's my guess." Tarik let one towel fall but balled the other one up and slam-dunked it to the ground.

"You mean I burned pieces of my boat *for nothing*?"

Tarik sighed. "I'm afraid so."

Sander's eyes blazed and his chest lifted. He raised both fists and punched the air in the direction of the disappearing plane. "*Fuck!*"

Tarik had never heard Sander utter that word, although it was certainly justified. He was about to lay an arm across Sander's shoulders, but then two things happened.

Tarik caught a snippet of a message. "*—on approach to Sitia, heading—*"

And the plane wobbled in the air.

Tarik goggled at the aircraft, although he really didn't give a shit about it anymore.

Beside him, Sander ass-planted in the sand. "I can't believe it," he said, his tone utterly defeated.

Tarik blinked down at him, at his dejected expression, at the droop of his shoulders. *At his hands.* "Neither can I," Tarik murmured.

"I wasn't taking this seriously, you know?" Sander grabbed fistfuls of sand and flung them aside. "I figured we just needed to hold out for a week, tops, and then Katalin would return, the gulls would give her the message, and we'd be home as soon as Luken could charter a sea plane. They'd probably send my cousin Otho along to let us know help was coming. But if no one knows where we are..." He raised a bleak face to Tarik. "What if nobody's coming? What if they intended for you to die here?"

Tarik dropped down next to Sander and took his hands— his incredible hands. "Hey. In case you hadn't noticed, I'm not the only one on this island."

"But think about it, Tarik. Whoever contracted Stormsurge and whatshername, Lightbender—they couldn't have known that I'd show up for my birthday cruise early."

Tarik blinked. "Birthday cruise? It's your birthday?"

"Next week."

"Why didn't you tell me?"

Sander lifted an eyebrow. "Because we've spent half our time sniping at each other and the other half in bed?" He tugged on his hands, although not as if he were really trying to escape Tarik's hold. "Besides, it doesn't matter. The point is that I shouldn't have been onboard. And if I hadn't shown up before the vandals could finish their job, you might have been stranded with nothing. With no way to survive. Alone." Sander's voice broke on the word. "As angry as I am about everything else, about the damage to *Askatasun*, about the irresponsibility of contract supos who don't follow up with their clients, that's something I can't forgive. That you might have been here by yourself." His voice dropped to a whisper. "That you might have died thinking it was my idea."

Tarik caressed Sander's cheek. "I wouldn't have made that leap in any case. I didn't know you had a boat, let alone what it was called."

"The Roses Estate kegs would have been a giveaway. Nobody but someone in my family would have access to the unbottled wine." He lifted devastated eyes to Tarik. "I can't bear that, Tarik. I can't."

"Shhh." Tarik leaned in and kissed Sander softly. "You don't have to. Because it didn't happen. We're here together, and that's a fucking good thing, because together we are going to get off this fucking island and kick the kidnapper's fucking ass."

Sander blinked at him. "How are we going to do that?"

"Easy." Tarik lifted their joined hands and kissed Sander's knuckles one at a time. "With these."

CHAPTER TEN

The frustration still buzzing under his skin didn't stop Sander from gaping at Tarik. "What are you talking about?"

"When did the thing happen? When you blew out the wiring in the Castle?"

Sander's belly clenched, and he tugged on his hands, but Tarik's grip only tightened. "You mean when I *killed my father*? Is that what you want to talk about now?"

"When, Sander. Do you remember the date?"

His fists clenched in Tarik's hold. "I could hardly forget. It was—"

"Seventeen years ago last November, right? November second?"

"How do you— You know what? Never mind." The ease Sander had begun to feel with Tarik, the closeness from last night, the feelings—God, the *feelings*. All of them were clearly an illusion. The Tarik that Sander believed he knew was just another facade of the Duke of Arse. "Please let go of me." He hoped his voice sounded cold and not heartbroken, but he held little hope for that. He'd always been a lousy actor.

And Tarik had zero right to look so devastated when he released Sander's hands, damn him.

"S-Sander?"

"Was this *your* plot all along? To pry the story out of me so you could taunt me with it later?"

Tarik threaded his hands through his curls and clutched them as though to yank them out. "That's not what—" He let go of his hair and reached for Sander again, but stopped when Sander flinched. "Listen. I know what happened. I know what set you off."

Sander wrapped his arms across his stomach. "How could you possibly know that?"

"Because it didn't affect only you. It got me too."

"Tarik—"

"No, just listen. Please. Listen?" Despite Tarik's obvious backsliding into asshole territory, Sander couldn't resist the plea in those midnight eyes. So he nodded.

Tarik paced in front of him, bare feet kicking up sand with the energy of his steps. "I was seventeen. My uncle had just bestowed my power moniker with all the pomp of that ridiculous ceremony and I thought I was hot shit." He shot a wry grin at Sander. "Modesty has never been one of my strengths."

Sander couldn't help a chuckle. "I can believe that."

"The headaches were already a problem, but not too bad. But then, on November second, there was a CME."

"A what?"

"A CME. Coronal mass ejection. The sun emits this surge of solar wind." He waved an impatient hand. "I'm not sure of the timing. Maybe it happened before the second, but it hit the earth then and created a massive geomagnetic storm. It damaged the Abarran communications satellite and the backlash from that absolutely flattened me. I was unconscious for three days and spent the next week floating in an immersion tank with the worst migraine ever." He stopped pacing and shrugged. "The headaches got worse after that."

"Tarik..." *God, I'm a fool.* But Sander couldn't help reaching out and gripping Tarik's shoulder, the skin warm under Sander's palm. "I'm sorry you went through that, but I don't see what it has to do with—"

"Don't you see?" Tarik pressed his own hand over Sander's. "Because of your affinity to the earth's magnetic fields, you acted like a... a lightning rod for the geomagnetic pulse. It fed power into you until you couldn't contain it, but you didn't *cause* it. You were a victim too, just like me." He gazed into Sander's eyes. "Just like your father."

Sander shook his head. "Even if you're right, it was still my fault. If I hadn't been there—"

"The fault, if there is any, lies with those idiots at the Ministry of Powers who never bothered to investigate your ability. Who left you twisting in the wind until you ended up as a casualty of a random act of God."

Sander's lips twitched. *Shit, do I actually want to smile?* But a seed of warmth had sprouted inside him, pushing through the guilt he carried with him always. "An act of God? You mean like, I don't know, a *drought*?"

Tarik groaned dramatically, but his eyes twinkled. "Throwing my dickhead behavior back at me now? I thought we'd gotten past all that."

"Even if what you say is true—"

"It is." Tarik's tone was fierce. "I will never lie to you, Sander. I promise." He gripped both Sander's shoulders. "Do you believe me?"

"Maybe it makes me a fool as well as a monster, but I do."

"Not a monster." Tarik drew him into a loose embrace that promised comfort rather than lust. "Never a monster."

With Tarik's arms around him, sheltering him, Sander was able to imagine a day when that would be true. "Thank you."

Tarik smiled at him and kissed his forehead. "Now. Are you ready to get off this fucking island?"

Was he? In a way, Sander wished they could stay. Not forever, but longer. Because after they returned to their respective countries, they'd never be allowed this closeness again. But that wouldn't be fair. Sander was used to isolation. Tarik wasn't. Besides, the diet of fish and emergency rations was already getting old, and the wine wouldn't last forever. So he nodded.

Tarik lifted one arm—Sander immediately missed his warmth—and pointed in the air. "Did you see what happened when you lost your temper at the plane?"

Sander scowled. "No. I was too busy wishing it a sudden collision with a flock of seagulls."

"You *spanked* it, Sander. You hit it with a magnetic wave and it wobbled in the air."

Sander tore himself out of Tarik's arms and stumbled backward. "You mean I *went off* on it?" His knees buckled, and he collapsed onto the sand. "I didn't really want it to crash. Oh, God, Tarik, what if I'd shorted out their guidance systems?"

Tarik dropped to his hands and knees and prowled toward him. "You didn't. And you know why?" Sander drew his knees to his chest and clasped his trembling hands around them, too mortified to get a word out but unable to tear his gaze away from Tarik's face. "The bucket."

"You're not making any sense. What does the bucket have to do with the plane? With me..." He swallowed against the bile rising in his throat. "With me killing someone else."

"Ah, fuck, baby." Tarik knelt in front of Sander, bracketing Sander's feet with his knees. "You didn't kill anyone, okay? Not even close. Because of the bucket. Because of what the bucket taught you. Because of what you *learned* from the bucket."

"How does hauling water—"

"Not water, Sander. *Control.*" Although Tarik's voice was low, it rang with excitement, with elation. "You know how to manipulate the magnetic field now, to regulate it, to make it answer to you. Since you weren't a conduit for the power of the fucking *sun* this time, you had only your own power to draw on. Are you listening? Because this is important."

"I can't very well ignore you," Sander grumbled. "You're sitting right in front of me." Which might be the only thing that was keeping him from flinging himself into the sea.

"Then hear this, Sander Fiala, Duke of Roses." Tarik's chest rose with his slow inhale. "Your leashed power, your intentional power, your *trained* power *isn't lethal.*" Tarik's mouth lifted in a lopsided grin. "Although I suspect it could be if you wanted."

"I don't. I wouldn't. Never again. I can't—"

"There's more." Tarik captured Sander's face between his hands, and the panic bubbling like acid in Sander's belly faded. "When you walloped the plane—"

"Please don't say that," Sander said faintly.

"All right. When you patted the plane—"

"Tarik." Sander glared at him. "That's not any better."

"Avoiding the truth won't make it go away." Tarik smoothed Sander's hair off his forehead. "That's the favorite trick of the fucking Ministry of Powers. They exiled you and brushed off their hands, congratulating themselves on a job well done instead of finding a solution.

"I'm pretty sure they thought they'd found the perfect solution," Sander said wryly.

"But that's my point. They didn't. They just put you out of their minds and called it done." Tarik edged closer. "They stole *years* from you, Sander. Productive years. Peaceful years." He gazed earnestly into Sander's eyes. "Guilt-free years. They let you suffer because they couldn't be bothered. If I were you, I'd want to do something about it.

Because if I were you…" He grinned, a decided glint in his eyes. "… I'd be royally pissed."

Sander's belly swooped like he'd missed the last step on the Manor staircase. *Could it be true?* Wonder, relief, excitement, anger—oh, most definitely anger—chased through him in dizzying chaos.

But woven through it all, like an unbreakable golden cord, a cord anchored to the man now peering at him from dark, worried eyes, was more.

Love.

Yes, it had happened fast, but Sander's life-altering events always happened quickly. The Disaster had changed everything in an instant. *But this was the inverse of the Disaster.*

The Miracle.

"Sander?"

The uncertainty in Tarik's voice woke Sander from his epiphany. He scrambled onto his knees and launched himself at Tarik, wrapping his arms around him and toppling both of them to the sand.

"*Ooof.*" Tarik smiled tentatively. "This is becoming your signature move."

"Is that a problem?"

He ran a finger along Sander's jaw. "Not fucking likely."

Sander kissed Tarik softly. *While I still can.* "Thank you. And you're right. I am royally pissed. At the Ministry. At whoever attacked you. At myself for letting everyone label me all these years."

Tarik laid a gentle finger on Sander's lips. "Not yourself. You were a child and the adults who should have had your best interests at heart failed you."

But you didn't. "So what should we do? Without another plane—"

"We don't need a plane. All we need is you." He grabbed Sander's left hand. "Positive pole." He captured the other. "Negative pole."

Sander narrowed his eyes. "Oookay. Not sure I'm following."

"I heard something, Sander. The pilot's transmission traveled along your magnetic pulse." His smile was brilliant. "If we combine our powers, we can get a message out. I'm sure of it."

Sander pulled away and sat up, his earlier joy fading under familiar self-doubt. "I've only been practicing for two days. What if I hurt someone?" *What if I hurt you?* "You said yourself that my power might be lethal if I wanted."

"But that's the thing. You don't want." Tarik pushed himself to his knees. "You're a craftsman, Sander. You build barrels. You built a fucking boat. You know more about precision than those ridiculous artists at the North Abarran Art Institute who paint entire landscapes on pin heads. You can do this. You can save us, sweetheart."

"Sweetheart? Don't you mean Monster?"

"No. Definitely not." Tarik smiled at Sander and stroked his cheek. "A total sweetheart, through and through." He kissed Sander, soft and lingering. "Now what do you say? Shall we give it a try? Because I've got to tell you, I've never been a fan of being a sitting duck."

Despite the panic leaping in his belly, Sander smirked. "Don't you mean a sitting duke?"

Tarik lifted both eyebrows. "So sassy. I like it."

Sander rose to his feet. "Okay. What do we need to do?"

Tarik squinted into the sky. "How far up would you say that plane was flying?"

"I don't know. Not very high. Maybe less than a kilometer?"

"We can't know how far Lightbender's field extends, but that doesn't really matter because my communication power doesn't rely on sight. All we need to do is get a good push off the island, enough to counteract my fucking surrounded-by-water weakness."

"I see a major flaw in this plan."

"You would. You're the most pessimistic man I've ever met."

Sander ignored the dig, just as he ignored the affection in Tarik's tone. "Even if we manage to send the message—"

"We will. I have faith in you." Tarik leaned closer, his voice dropping to a suggestive murmur. "Even if you have none in yourself."

Okay, major melting going on here. Everywhere except my cock. "F-fine. We'll postulate the message sent. But how do we know it'll be received by someone who can do something about it? Or for that matter, by anyone at all?"

Tarik waved one elegant hand. "There's a dedicated receiver in my office that's calibrated for my messages. It's a requirement for maintaining my power moniker and validating my contracts as Wavelength. All messages that I personally transmit have to be recorded, so there's no hint of impropriety or contract breach."

"Can you send a message that far?" Heat rushed up Sander's throat. "I don't mean to insult you. I don't know anything about your range, that's all."

Tarik cupped the back of Sander's neck. "I'm not insulted. It's a fair question." He pressed a soft kiss to Sander's lips. "When it comes to receiving, I've got a range that's about three times the reach of the average cell tower. But as for sending? Let's put it this way. I transmitted from Hollywood when I was at the Oscar ceremony last year and it came through just fine. If we can get it out, it'll be received, and it'll ping my assistant's alerts. You don't need to worry about the other end. Let's concentrate on our job here."

"So the signal can *cross* water?"

"Yes. As long as it's not blocked at the source"—he pointed to himself—"the airwaves will carry it." He held out a hand and Sander took it. "Ready?"

Sander nodded. "Where, um..." He glanced around. "Where would be the best place to do this? On the cliff near the waterfall?"

Tarik frowned up at the rocks, his head tilted to one side. "That's where you've had the most practice, but for some reason that feels wrong." He scanned the beach, his gaze lighting on *Askatasun*. "There. Let's try it from your boat. The place you feel most comfortable, the most centered, the most at home."

The place where I fell in love with my enemy.

One way or another, once they were rescued—and they *would* be rescued, Sander was determined on it, for Tarik's sake if not for his own—he was sending someone back to retrieve *Askatasun*. He might never sail her again. He might never repair her, just keep her in dry dock. Maybe build her a special boathouse all her own, somewhere he could spend time aboard, remembering the feel of Tarik's hands on his skin, Tarik's taste on his tongue, Tarik's cock in his hand.

Because that was the downside of being rescued. The world outside this island—the real world—held no place they could be together.

So Sander let Tarik lead him across the sand and climbed up onto *Askatasun*'s lazarette, facing out to sea over the stern. "What do you want me to do?"

"When you spanked the plane—"

Sander groaned. "I told you not to say that."

Tarik grinned. "Why not? It's descriptive. You smacked it right on its tail." He took Sander's hands and folded them into fists, gripping them with his own. "You sort of punched the air. Emphatically."

"Like when I sent the cable saw flying the first time?"

"Exactly like that, but you don't have to send an object. The magnetic pulse will do the job on its own."

"How will you piggyback onto it then?"

Tarik smiled wryly. "Guess I'll have to practice. The radio frequencies I detect and use are in the electromagnetic spectrum, and I can tell the difference between them within a few hertz. I'll just have to learn what your magnetic pulses feel like." He turned Sander to face him, gripping his shoulders. "But if you get tired, if this drains you, just say the word and we'll stop."

"If hauling countless buckets of water didn't drain me, I doubt carrying nothing but your message will do the trick. Ready?"

"Absolutely. I don't want to overload the message, so I'll keep it succinct. What's our approximate location?"

Sander gave Tarik the coordinates and turned in the direction of home—because now that he knew what he was sensing, the reason he could navigate without instruments, he had no trouble targeting it.

Sander took a deep breath and held it, closing his eyes, imagining the swirl of magnetic force under him, over him, around him and *punched* with both fists.

Nothing happened.

"Shit." He stared at his hands. "I don't think that went anywhere. Without an object to move, it's impossible to tell."

Tarik's face lit up. "Just a minute." He jumped to the ground and raced to the blanket next to the fire, peering at the ground until he must have found what he was seeking. He grabbed something and held up his fist in triumph, and his smile, the light in his eyes, the sun in his hair, caught in Sander's chest like a fishhook, reeling him in tighter than ever.

He made himself take breaths, forcing down the impulse to blurt *I love you* as Tarik ran back and climbed aboard.

Because this wasn't the time or place. *There might never be the time or place. Not for us.* But he pushed that thought away too.

"Here." Tarik opened his hand to display the half dozen nails Sander had stripped from *Askatasun*'s splintered hull before tossing the wood into the fire. "Use these. They'll let you gauge how far you're reaching until you get the feel for it." He shaded his eyes, peering out at the sea. "I'll be able to track it too and figure out how to latch onto it."

"All right." Sander selected one of the nails from Tarik's open palm. "Could you— Would you hold on to my shoulder while I do this? Please? It helps."

Tarik's expression of triumph softened. "It does?"

"Yes. You… you ground me." *And I don't want to lose any chance to feel your touch.*

"Then I'm happy to do it." Tarik gripped Sander's shoulder, his palm warm and smooth against Sander's skin, and turned them to face the water. "Ready when you are, Your Grace."

Four nails and one alarming misstep later, something shifted in Sander's perception, as if he'd been staring at a sea chart upside down and suddenly righted it. The next nail sailed so far out from shore that they lost sight of it before it fell into the waves. Sander shared a grin with Tarik, but Tarik didn't let him rest.

"Try it again, only without the nail."

Sander did. "I'm pretty sure that one got *somewhere*."

Tarik's hand tightened on Sander's shoulder. "They've all gotten somewhere. But please. Once more for me?"

Sander couldn't deny the plea, the hope in Tarik's eyes. So he set his jaw and faced the sea. *Once more. For us.*

This time, as Tarik squeezed his shoulder in time with the punch, Sander could swear he traveled along with the pulse, his heart flying over the water and arrowing straight for home.

"Perfect," Tarik murmured, and kissed Sander's neck. "We'll send another every hour on the hour because nobody has ever accused me of being subtle. Now." He turned Sander toward him and snaked an arm around his waist. "We've fifty-nine minutes and twenty-seven seconds before the next transmission." He pulled Sander flush against his body, his hard cock a brand against Sander's own. "However will we pass the time?"

Sander's mouth on Tarik's dick was... *ungh!* Tarik sucked in a breath, which was fucking hard to do with his nose buried in Sander's balls. *Not yet. Not yet.* "Sander," he gasped.

But Sander didn't heed the warning. He sucked Tarik deeper, although he writhed when Tarik crooked the finger buried in his ass and brushed his prostate. And that moan... *Fuck. "Sander!"*

Fire sparked along Tarik's spine and his vision whited out as he came in Sander's mouth. Somehow he retained enough brain cells to twist his fingers in Sander's ass again as he licked a stripe up Sander's dick. Before he could take it in his mouth, though, Sander shot all over Tarik's face and hair.

"God, Tarik," Sander gasped. "I'm sorry."

Laughing, Tarik rolled onto his back and pressed a kiss to Sander's hip. "For what? For sucking my brains out my dick for the fourth time since yesterday? Because let me tell you, that's nothing to apologize for." He sat up, careful not to get too enthusiastic and whack his head on the cabin top again. "Although next time we're stranded on a deserted island, remember to pack condoms."

Tarik grimaced, ducking his head so his hair hid his expression. *Next time.* Rescue was bound to come soon because Tarik was absolutely certain his messages had gotten out, riding over the waves on Sander's rock-solid magnetic pulses. There wouldn't be a next time for them. There couldn't. As enemies both politically and economically, neither of their governments was likely to countenance a friendship between them, let alone anything more. Not without cries of treason and accusations of compromising national security.

Tarik peeked through the screen of his hair. Sander's earlier blissed-out smile had faded into one tinged with sadness and wry affection that gutted Tarik as though he were one of those hapless fish. Because Sander wasn't a fool. He knew as well as Tarik did that their relationship was bounded by their island prison. *And, fuck, it is a relationship, isn't it?* Something Tarik had never seen coming when he faced Sander on top of a hill among withering grapevines and seen only the Monster, not the man.

"Tarik?"

"Hmmm?"

"If you want to take a shower—"

Tarik caught Sander's hand and kissed each finger. "No. I don't want you to spend all day hauling water again. I'll take a morning dip. After all—" He forced heartiness into his tone. "—rescue is bound to arrive today."

"Right." Sander set his jaw as if he were bracing for a body blow. "Rescue."

Tarik crawled out of bed and padded to the galley sink. He used the foot pump to run water over a clean cloth, amazed again at *Askatasun*'s convenience, at the care, *the love*, that Sander had crafted into every snug corner of his boat. He took it back to Sander. "Here. You're not quite as messy as I am."

Sander smiled up at him, more mischievous than sorrowful. "This time, anyway."

Leaving Sander to clean himself up, Tarik fled through the companionway and practically dove off the deck to sprint down to the water. He waded into the surf, the water raising goosebumps on his skin. *Next time, we're getting stranded in the South Pacific where the water stands a chance of being as warm as my bath.*

Next time? *Fuck.*

Tarik ducked under the waves, because he seriously needed to soak his head. Was he *still* dreaming of a next time?

Why, yes. Yes, he was. *Talk about a giant cosmic bitch-slap.* He'd been so arrogant, confident he could make any match work, whatever Bastien needed—whatever *North Abarra* needed—because he'd never imagined this could happen to him.

He'd never imagined falling in love.

Damn it, Bas was right. Tarik had gotten to know Sander and *pow.* Attraction and affection—*love*—had taken him down for the count.

But Bastien was also wrong. Because none of the endless stream of "eligible" matches had ever stirred the least desire in Tarik to get to know them better. None of the others were as talented, as determined, as selfless as Alesander Fiala, Duke of Roses.

Nobody else could possibly touch Tarik's heart now. *Although if I ever hear anybody call him Monster again, I will touch* them, all right—with my fist in their face.

He submerged, swimming underwater until his lungs burned and he had to explode onto the surface to catch his breath. He turned onto his back, rocked by the gentle swells, and stared up at the sky as the rising sun turned it from pearl gray to blush pink.

There had to be some way for them to be together. Some way that wouldn't compromise the political stability of both their countries, not to mention their own safety. Because there were factions in North Abarra that would be thrilled, not to say rabid, about toppling Bastien off the throne, and

Tarik was too experienced a politician himself to think the same wasn't also true in South Abarra. It didn't matter who was in power, or how benevolent or populist their rule. Somebody always wanted to replace them.

He sighed and righted himself to slosh onto shore, then stopped. *Fuck. I forgot a towel.* Oh well. Yesterday's was still draped over the gunwale on the other side of *Askatasun*, rescued from Tarik's impromptu semaphore act yesterday. Tarik wasn't so fussy and pampered that he couldn't use the same towel more than once.

He chuckled as he circled the boat, a warm breeze playing across his skin and no doubt making a right bird's nest of his hair, but so what? Nobody would see him but Sander, and Tarik knew Sander wouldn't care. In fact, if he was lucky—if they were both lucky—Sander would mess it up even more before rescue arrived.

Tarik increased his pace and rounded *Askatasun*'s stern. *Oh yeah. We're definitely getting lucky again before—*

A man stood near the bow. And it wasn't the ludicrous outfit the guy was sporting that stopped Tarik in his tracks, jaw sagging. *Neon green spandex? Really?* Nor the bedazzled messenger bag at his hip—*dude, fanny packs went out in the nineties.* Nor the way his lemon yellow cape fanned out behind him in opposition to the wind's direction.

No. It was the self-satisfied smirk as he viewed the boulder that penetrated Sander's beloved boat, his arms folded across his rather concave chest. *Spandex is definitely not a good choice for this guy.*

He caught sight of Tarik and his eyes widened.

Right. Naked. Tarik snatched his target towel and wrapped it around his waist. "Morning."

"So, Wavelength." The guy propped his hands on his hips and struck a pose. "Your wicked plan failed miserably, as I knew it would."

"I see you know who I am." Tarik willed Sander to come out on deck—and then thought better of it. If this guy was another unaffiliated supo with a contract on one or both of them, he wanted Sander well out of the fight. "Afraid I can't return the favor."

The guy's chest rose, although not very far, and his cheeks and neck turned an alarming shade of puce below the edge of his mask. "I am Deliverer. And I am here to ensure that you answer for your crimes."

"Which crimes would those be? Because I've got to tell you, this crime against fashion"—he gestured to Deliverer's outfit—"might be a capital offense."

"Silence!" He pointed at Tarik, his hand encased in a green spandex gauntlet with enough crystals on the cuff to outfit a debutante ball. "You murdered the Duke of Roses and then tried to escape in his boat. You could never hope to get away with such a thing. And you have not!" He spread his hands to indicate the island. "Behold your prison. Your place of exile. The last home you will ever know."

"Otho?" Sander's quizzical voice startled Deliverer into a slapstick-worthy double-take. "It worked then? Our message got through?"

Deliverer gaped. "Sander? But they were supposed to—" He glanced behind him as if he expected somebody else to magically show up. "Wh-what are you doing here?"

Sander jumped onto the sand, a sunny grin on his face. "Waiting for rescue, of course." He hurried over to stand beside Tarik, close enough for their shoulders to brush. "Tarik, this is my cousin Otho. I told you Katalin and Luken would probably send him ahead of everyone else." He turned back to his cousin. "So when will the plane arrive?"

Instead of returning Sander's smile, Deliverer-slash-Otho's lips twisted in a sneer. "Never!"

Next to Tarik, Sander tensed. "What do you mean?"

"I *mean*, that even though you've nearly ruined everything as usual, the plan is proceeding like clockwork."

"Plan?" Sander's eyes turned as hard as the stones littering the sand. "Did you know about this, Otho? Were you part of it all along?" Sander was practically vibrating. "Did you kidnap Tarik? Are you the one who hurt him?"

"Babe." Tarik placed a hand on Sander's arm. "I don't think—"

"'Babe?' *'Babe?'*" Otho's voice rose in a screech. "Do you mean to tell me that on top of *everything else*, you actually *consorted* with him? He's the enemy!" Otho waved a spandex-covered hand at Tarik. "And you're the... the..."

"The what, Otho?" Sander's voice was low and deadly. "The Monster of Roses? The man nobody would dare touch?"

"Monster of Roses." Otho snorted. "All these years, people feared you for *nothing*. But *I* knew." He thumped his thin chest. "*I* knew you were a phony martyr, an ineffectual coward. A shirker. Sailing away whenever things got difficult. Never stepping up to offer your services for the *greater good!*"

Tarik edged toward Sander. "Does he always speak in italics and exclamation points?"

Sander glanced sidelong at him. "Pretty much, yeah."

Tarik rolled his eyes. "Ridiculous. And 'Deliverer' has to be the worst power moniker ever."

"It's not real. Aunt Maialen never granted him one."

"Shut up!" Otho's shout brought their attention back to him and—fuck—the rising sun glinted off the blue steel of the gun in his hand. "She never granted you one either. Everyone calls you the Monster, even though you're not worthy, so why can't I pick my own, too?"

Sander laced his fingers with Tarik's, both their hands sweatier than the cool morning merited. "I never wanted that name, even though I earned it." Sander's voice sank on the last words, and Tarik turned to him, gripping his shoulders.

"You never deserved that name."

"Exactly!" Otho brandished his gun. "I've been saying that for *years*!"

The devastation in Sander's eyes threatened to break Tarik's heart in two. "I thought you meant that in a completely different way, Otho. I thought we were friends."

"Friends," Otho spat. "A *friend* would have advocated for me with his precious aunt. A *friend* would have— You know what? Never mind." He raised the gun, his hand wobbling. "Even if *you're* not, *I'm* not afraid to take the bold step. To challenge the way things have been. To pave the way for *a brilliant future!*"

"But if you received the message, then everyone knows this was all a mistake."

He smirked. "Ah, but 'you' is the operative word. *Me.* Not 'everybody.'"

Tarik shared a mystified glance with Sander. "No wonder your aunt never granted him a power moniker. If he's this bad at explaining himself, he must be a fucking terrible courier."

"Shut up, shut up, shut *up!*" He brandished the gun. "I can *block* messages as well as deliver them." He jerked his chin up. "Take *that*, Wavelength."

"Uh…" Tarik screwed up his face. "Take what?"

"When your stupid assistant called the Castle, nobody would let him talk to the Queen. Instead, since I'm the Royal Courier, they put him through to me."

"You mean…" Sander's fingers tightened on Tarik's. "They don't know? Aunt Maialen. Katalin. Luken. They don't know where I am?"

He puffed out his chest again. "Only me. And some lowly assistant at a North Abarran vineyard." He scoffed. "As if anybody would listen to him. *He's* not a Royal."

Tarik edged closer to Sander, so their shoulders were brushing. "Did *you* tell anybody? Since you are the Royal Courier and all."

Otho smiled primly. "Not yet. Not until I've got the *right* message." He raised the gun. "You, Wavelength, attacked my cousin and then stole his boat. But since you have no idea how to sail, you wrecked it on this island. After days of vile captivity, my cousin managed to wrestle your gun away and shoot you." He gripped the gun with both hands, but it still wavered so much that Tarik was afraid the idiot would shoot Sander by mistake.

Not an option. Keep him monologuing.

As much as he hated to, Tarik let go of Sander's hand so he could put a little distance between them. "I see a few flaws in your plan."

"There are no flaws!" Otho glowered at Sander. "Even though Sander nearly screwed everything up. Like he always does."

"No flaws, eh? How is he supposed to shoot me if I murdered him before I took the boat?"

Otho blinked rapidly, as if that had never occurred to him. But then his mouth firmed. "Never mind that. When Sander's body washes up on shore with his head bashed in, everyone will know you killed him and dumped him overboard."

"So he shot me after I coshed him and tossed him in the drink?" He chuckled and used the distraction to take a couple more steps from Sander. "Fuck, he's more talented than I thought, and I think he's pretty fucking talented."

"Tarik." Sander sounded as if he'd forced Tarik's name from between clenched teeth.

For the first time in his life, Tarik received a message loud and clear without needing his power at all. He tilted his head, a derisive smile on his face as he looked Otho up and down. "You're the biggest idiot in Abarra, North or South, if you think for an instant that Sander's not worth every fucking honor anyone could throw at him. You have no idea who you're dealing with, asshole." His smile stretched to a grin. "But you're about to find out."

"Stop talking!" Otho's aim drifted toward Sander. "You're trying to confuse me, and it won't work. The plan —"

The gun jerked out of Otho's grip and with one sweep of Sander's arms, sailed out to sea and vanished into the water with a distant *plop*.

CHAPTER ELEVEN

For a moment, Sander let his arms hang in the air, amazed that his hands weren't shaking. If he hadn't been able to focus, if Otho had gotten off a shot, if Tarik had been injured, or worse, died...

Disaster.

He lowered his arms and faced Otho, whose mouth was hanging open like a basking shark's. Heated anger roiled in Sander's belly. How could he have been so mistaken all this time? For almost his entire life?

"Otho," he ground out between clenched molars. "Do you really hate me enough to murder me?"

Otho was still staring at his hands, as if he couldn't believe the gun was gone. "I wasn't— That was him. Supposed to be him."

"You mean Tarik?"

"No. I mean yes. I mean..." Otho launched himself into the air, but he hadn't gone five meters before he was swarmed by a flock of seagulls—pecking at his face, shitting in his hair, and plucking at his stupid cape. *"Auuuuggghhh! Get them off! Get them off!"*

Sander grinned at Tarik. "The message got through to South Abarra too. Because that—" He pointed to the seagull attack squad. "—is definitely my sister's work."

Tarik sauntered over and wrapped an arm around Sander's waist. "How does his cape do that? The wind is in a completely different quarter."

Sander snorted. "He had the tailor... Hunh." His grinned widened, and he nuzzled behind Tarik's ear. "Watch me work."

Sander raised his hands, the swirl of the field around them familiar now, almost like wood he could shape to his will. He latched onto the metal piping in Otho's cape and *yanked*, sending it plummeting down to wedge deep in the sand, with Otho sprawled red-faced and gasping atop what Sander hoped were several extremely pointy rocks. The seagulls, although they couldn't see through Lightbender's shield, didn't stop pooping, and most of their, er, offerings, found a target.

Tarik squinted down at Otho. "Do you suppose this was really all his doing?"

"I doubt it." Sander raised an eyebrow. "Do you?"

"Not a chance. Not after the world's most convoluted and contradictory monologue." Tarik kicked sand in Otho's direction. "He's obviously nothing but a stooge."

"I'm not! It's my plan. I'm totally in charge," Otho croaked, nearly getting a mouthful of seagull shit for his trouble. "They'll celebrate my name in the street when—"

"When what?" Tarik crouched down, although he didn't either let go of Sander or move into seagull-poop range. "When we tell everyone we know what a fucking incompetent supervillain you are? I doubt you'd warrant as much as a sock puppet on Bonfire Night."

Otho glared at them. "You'll see. This isn't over."

Sander glanced out to sea, where the noise of more than one engine approached in the brightening dawn. "Actually, Otho, I think it is." *But I'm not sure I want it to be.*

Because what chance did he have to be with Tarik anywhere else but on this island? Not in South Abarra, where Wavelength was vilified from top government circles to the lowest criminal underworld in South Dulibre. Not in North Abarra, where Sander was and always would be the Monster of Roses. Nowhere in either country, countries they each loved, countries where they had responsibilities. Sander wasn't the kind of man—and he was certain Tarik wasn't either—who could put personal desire ahead of duty and emigrate to someplace that wouldn't care about their royal blood or royal powers.

Royal powers. That was another wrinkle. Tarik wouldn't step away from his Wavelength contracts. He couldn't. They were too valuable to his country, to his king, to his family. And would the Ministry of Powers accept that Sander was fully in control now—at least provided he could be adequately shielded from random geomagnetic storms? Would his own duties increase now? Would he be pulled into court intrigue and influence jockeying? Hell, would he be expected to enter into a political marriage like his grandfather's?

Sander's belly turned over, unsettled as it had never been at sea. How could he live without seeing Tarik's smile every day, without threading his fingers through those soft curls, without the taste of Tarik's kiss?

He turned away from Otho and faced the oncoming aircraft. *Three of them. One for me. One for Tarik.* He glanced back at his cousin—*second cousin*. And one for Otho.

Tarik flanked Sander, his gaze on the planes too. "There are a lot of things I regret about this, Sander. That your boat was wrecked. That you were frightened and worried. That you found out your cousin—"

"Second cousin."

"Second cousin was an asshole. Fuck, that *I* was an asshole for way too long." Tarik rested his hand, light and warm, in the small of Sander's back. "But I will never, *ever*, regret you. Knowing you. Being with you. Lo—" He leaned his forehead against Sander's shoulder for an instant. "Don't forget that, okay? Don't forget that for a little while, we were each other's world." He lifted his head and his whisper was almost drowned by the seaplanes—two with the Queen's crest and one with the North Abarran king's coat of arms—as they landed one by one on an ocean that was suddenly as smooth as glass. "Because I never will. No matter what."

Then Tarik stepped away, leaving at least two meters of space between them as inflatable rafts deployed from all three planes. *I was right. One for me. One for Tarik. And one for Otho.* Sander set his jaw. *At least I'll make sure those incredibly burly guards arrest the correct person, and that Otho's accusations don't implicate Tarik in any way.*

The North Abarran contingent arrived first. "This way, Your Grace," their leader said, moving to place his body between Tarik's and Sander's, with a brief, startled glance at Otho still being bombarded by the seagulls. They hustled him away and into their raft before Katalin and Luken reached shore. He was still wearing nothing but a towel.

He didn't look back.

"Oh my God, Sander." Katalin grabbed him around the neck in a stranglehold, and he hugged her back. Because the only way he'd get through losing Tarik, get through Otho's betrayal—although that was a far less lethal wound—was by depending on the people he was certain would never fail him. "When the gulls couldn't find you, I was so worried." She stepped back and cast a look of loathing at Otho. "I've always known Otho was a loathly worm but I never realized he was a *homicidal, treasonous* loathly worm."

"Not so much of the treason talk, okay?" He peered out at the North Abarran plane, which might as well be sitting on tarmac with the unnaturally calm sea. The waves had even stopped lapping at the shore. "I assume you contacted Stormsurge for this landing weather."

"Yes. We didn't even have to pay him. He said he never knew about the plot. The clients presented it as a way for them to escape for a romantic interlude without family interference." *Well, they got that right.* "He, um, says sorry about the boat. He's sending a crew to salvage her and take her back to our boathouse." She peered up at *Askatasun*. "Luken says he'll stay with you until they can get a suitably untechnical boat out here to collect you. I'll stay too. I don't mind."

Sander blinked. *Of course. I forgot.* Until this, er, *romantic interlude*, he hadn't been on a plane since before he hit puberty and started frying any electronics within a three-meter radius. "Actually, Kat, I can go with you on the plane. I've... discovered a few things about myself in the last few days. Watch."

He levitated the bucket which he'd discarded on the sand yesterday so he could kiss Tarik and sent it flying through the air. He was tempted to bonk Otho's head with it, but resisted. *Because I'm not the Monster anymore.*

Katalin clasped her hands under her chin, her eyes shining like the sea. "*Sander.* You can control your powers?"

"Let's say I understand them enough not to be a danger to myself or others." He smiled wryly as Tarik climbed aboard the North Abarran plane with his usual lithe grace, despite his less than regal outfit. "Do you suppose the pilot will believe that?"

Luken inclined his head. "If he won't, he's welcome to say here with *Askatasun* and let *me* fly the plane."

"Luken," Sander said with admiration. "You can fly planes too?"

"I can do many things, Your Grace. But now, my most pressing duty is to get you home safely."

So Sander let himself be bundled onto the raft and loaded onto a plane. He sat in the seat farthest from the cockpit and pressed his palm against the tiny window, because pressing his nose against it for a last glance at the island where he'd been so happy would have been pathetic. Someone touched his elbow, and he jerked, but it was only Luken, crouched under the low ceiling of the plane, holding out a tumbler which, from the smoky aroma, held Macallan on the rocks.

"Sir, we're about to take off. If you don't mind my saying so, you look as if you need this."

I look as if I need Tarik. "Thank you, Luken, but water would be preferable."

"Of course, sir." He turned away to take the two steps toward a small refrigerator.

Katalin reached across the aisle for him and Sander took her hand. "I'm so glad we found you, Sander. Mother and Aunt Maialen were beside themselves—and since Auntie can *literally* be beside herself, things got a little crowded in our wing of the Castle." She chuckled. "I've never seen her manifest so many ancillaries at once. The staff was going crazy trying to figure out which one to serve tea to."

In the window behind Katalin's head, Sander caught the movement of the North Abarran plane taking off, and it was if his heart was being wrenched out of his chest to trail along after it like an ad banner. "I..." He frowned, tracking the plane as it banked. "How *did* you find me, Kat? I mean, I recognized your handiwork with the seagulls, but how did you know to send them after Otho?"

She let go of his hand. It might have been because Luken returned with Sander's water—iced, in a crystal highball glass, and Sander longed briefly (and stupidly) for a dented metal bucket. But Sander had known Katalin her whole life and he could tell when she was hiding something.

"Kat," he said, his tone laced with warning.

"Don't blame Her Highness, sir," Luken said as he settled into the jump seat behind Katalin. "I take full responsibility."

"Responsibility for what?"

"For treason, of course," Luken said placidly. "For consorting with the North without permission."

Consorting. Sander and Tarik had been consorting all night long, and furthermore, he wished they still were. He narrowed his eyes, glancing between Luken's bland expression and Katalin's wary one. "You both might as well come clean. Because fuck that treason shit."

Katalin's eyes popped wide. "Sander! I've never heard you speak like that."

"If you don't tell me the truth, you're about to hear a lot more of it." He was dimly aware of the pilot speaking into his headset as he got ready to take off, but he swiveled to face his sister and valet. "I know for a fact that the message with our whereabouts went to Tarik's office in North Abarra."

Her eyebrows rose nearly to her hairline. "'Tarik?'"

Sander ignored the glee in her tone. "I also know, because Otho is an idiot who can't keep his mouth shut, that he intercepted an attempt to deliver the message to Castle Abarra. So how did you find out?"

Katalin's gaze slid away. "Weeeeellll…"

Sander reached across and squeezed her shoulder. "I'm not going to punish anybody, for God's sake. Just tell me what happened."

Luken crossed his legs and folded his hands on his knee, the picture of a perfectly well-bred gentleman. *He's more suited to being a duke than I am.* "After Nico—that is, Mr. Pereira—spoke with the Honorable Mr. Otho—"

"More like *dis*honorable," Katalin muttered.

"He didn't feel… confident that help would be forthcoming in an appropriate manner."

Sander lifted an eyebrow. "So he knows Otho, eh?"

"I couldn't say for certain, sir, but Mr. Pereira immediately called me at Roses Manor to deliver the information."

Sander frowned. "You? You personally, or you because you happened to answer the phone?"

For the first time since Sander had known Luken, he looked uncomfortable. "Me personally. We, ah, both owe our positions to the Municipal which keeps an up-to-date contact list for their placements."

"And then Luken came straight to me." Katalin patted Sander's hand. "While he was arranging for the plane, I called Otho."

"God, Kat, tell me you didn't ask for his help."

"Oh, no." Her eyes took on a steely glint, the same as when she confronted an elephant poacher. "I invited him to brunch."

Sander barked a laugh. "Let me guess. He turned you down."

She nodded, a wicked twist to her mouth. "And he *never* turns down brunch at the Manor, not with Chef Paul's cinnamon-orange buns on the menu. And *especially* not with the ridiculous excuse he trotted out."

"Which was?"

"He had to visit his tailor."

"To be fair, I think he actually did visit his tailor. He was wearing a rather more embellished costume just now." *Although it's significantly worse for wear thanks to the seagulls and me.*

She peered at him. "Did it have a cape?"

Sander nodded. "Yep. With the same metal piping to hold it in place." The better to hold Otho in place too. "Does Aunt Maialen know?"

"About Otho? Yes. About... about..."

"Our collusion with the North," Luken inserted smoothly, "no."

Sander's fists bunched. "It wasn't *collusion*. It was *cooperation*. And it saved our lives, mine and Tarik's, as well as preventing an incident that could have plunged us into war again." Katalin's seatbelt was still loose in her lap. Sander lifted his hands—*north pole and south pole*—and inserted the tongue into the buckle with a click.

Katalin stared down at it and then across at him. "S-Sander?"

"Best tighten that up, Kat." He settled back in his seat and took a swig of his ice water. "I predict turbulence ahead. Havoc. Turmoil. Upheaval. Perhaps a touch of mayhem." He smiled out her window at the disappearing North Abarran plane. "All of it intentional, for a change." *And all of it under perfect control.*

CHAPTER TWELVE

"Your Grace? I know you're busy, but…"

At Nico's tentative voice, Tarik looked up from his tablet screen. *Ah yes. God forbid actual work should interrupt my busy moping schedule.* For the last half hour, he'd been doing nothing but staring at the photograph of Sander, lifting his hand in a wave as he walked into Castle Abarra at the side of Prince Zorion.

"Don't worry about it." Tarik smiled at his assistant, who was about to get a massive promotion if Tarik had anything to say about it. "What can I do for you?"

Nico blinked, probably because that didn't describe their dynamic, did it? Usually Nico was the one doing things for Tarik, up to and including saving his life and the life of the man Tarik had finally admitted he was in love with. "Er, there's someone here to see you."

Tarik's heart gave an odd sideways jolt. *Sander.* He scrambled gracelessly to his feet. "Is it—"

"The King."

His heart settled down with a thump. "Ah. Thank you, Nico. Please show him in."

He remained standing as Nico ushered Bastien into the office. As soon as Nico bowed himself out, closing the door behind him, Tarik strode forward into Bastien's embrace. Bastien held onto him a few seconds longer, just as he had when he'd greeted the plane when Tarik landed last week. Tarik understood the impulse—he'd held on just as long, grateful to be back while at the same time needing the comfort of Bastien's arms when he was missing Sander so desperately.

When Bastien released him—you always waited for the King to make the first move—Tarik gestured to the chair by the window. "Please, sit." When Bastien settled, as regal as if the chair were his elaborate, hand-carved throne and not a leather wingback, Tarik took his own place on the sofa opposite him. "I'm always happy to see you, Bas, but usually I come to you. What brings you out of your prison? Oh, sorry. Did I say that? I meant your very comfortable and convenient—not to mention expensive—palace?"

Bastien's mouth lifted in a sardonic smile. "You're lucky I don't demand you occupy your quarters there permanently after this latest escapade."

"You can hardly blame me for getting kidnapped."

"Can't I? Only you, Tarik. Only you would get yourself kidnapped and marooned with Queen Maialen's *nephew*. Do you realize how close we came to declaring war to get you back?"

Tarik licked his dry lips. "Wh-what stopped you?"

"Two things." Bastien held up one long, elegant finger, seemingly not impeded by the heavy North Abarran royal signet. "First, that you'd told me about the message snippets you received, the ones that hinted at a plot. At first, I believed those foretold exactly what had happened—that the Monster of Roses—"

"Don't call him that," Tarik barked. Then he ran a hand over his face. *Don't bark commands at the King, you idiot, even if he is your cousin and best friend.*

"Your pardon. That the *Duke* of Roses had somehow gotten his hands on you."

Oh, he got his hands on me, all right. If only they were on me now. "And the second thing?"

"Ah, the second thing." He steepled his fingers, his eyes glinting with amusement, damn him. "That would be the demand from Queen Maialen that we return her nephew immediately or suffer the consequences."

"So you knew we were both missing right away."

"Soon enough. We had already begun a discreet search." He grimaced. "Although we had to keep it *very* discreet or risk igniting a furor demanding war on your behalf regardless of facts." He crossed his legs, his black trousers not daring to ride up. They were always perfectly creased, too, no matter how long Bastien had been wearing them that day. Tarik had no idea how he managed it. Maybe it was a second royal power. "For some incomprehensible reason, you're very popular with our people, despite your appalling temper and execrable company manners."

"Two reasons actually, neither all that incomprehensible." Tarik chuckled when Bastien pinched the bridge of his nose. "First, they're afraid I'll eavesdrop on their conversations—although why they think I'd have the time, let alone the inclination, since most conversations are incredibly tedious, I have no idea."

"And the second?"

Tarik spread his hands, indicating the vines marching down the hill outside the window as well as the office and the winery beyond. "I make their favorite wines."

"Touché."

"You still haven't told me why you're here."

Bastien extracted a folded paper from the inner pocket of his suit coat. "I received this from Queen Maialen today, and I'm rather annoyed, to be honest."

Tarik's blood seemed to abandon his head. Was this about Sander? Had something happened to him? "Annoyed? Why?"

"Annoyed that I didn't think of it first." He languidly unfolded the paper—parchment, glistening with the seal of South Abarra. "This is the notification that she is awarding the Mixtel Cross to—"

"To San— To the Duke of Roses?"

Bastien fixed him with a speculative gaze. "The Mixtel Cross is an honor for civilians, not Royals. Their highest, if I'm not mistaken. Their equivalent of our Northern Hope Medal."

"Right." Tarik smoothed his own trousers over his knee. *Wrinkled, damn it.* "I knew that."

"Just so. This particular award is being granted to your assistant, Nico Pereira."

"Nico?" Tarik carded his fingers through his hair. "But no North Abarran has ever been awarded the Mixtel Cross. It's strictly a South Abarran honor."

"Indeed. However, she believes it's warranted in this case for Mr. Pereira's critical part in the rescue of her nephew." He flicked the air with the fingers of his right hand. "Oh, and you, of course, but you were only mentioned tangentially in the text."

"That's... that's phenomenal." Tarik swallowed tightly, gripping the sofa arm. "He deserves it."

"He does. As I said, I consider myself delinquent in not coming to a similar conclusion myself. So, in response to a very polite letter from Her Majesty, I'm awarding the Northern Hope Medal to both Mr. Pereira and to Joseba Luken, the Duke of Roses' valet." He held up a hand to forestall Tarik's words. "Yes, I'm well aware that I'll catch untold shit from Parliament for awarding the medal to someone not on their nominee list, let alone someone from South Abarra, but you know what, Tarik?" Bastien's eyes glittered. "I don't. Fucking. Care."

"Bas—"

"Do you realize this is the first time—in my memory certainly, and possibly in centuries—when citizens of North and South Abarra have worked together to *avert* a war? To save important people on both sides of the border? It's a bloody miracle, and I'm ashamed I didn't see it for that before. Now." He sat back, his hands resting on the chair arms, a smug smile playing on his lips. "Is there something else you'd like to tell me?"

Raised voices from outside the door prevented Tarik from admitting to Bastien what he'd barely admitted to himself—that he loved Sander to the depths of his soul. Tarik took the reprieve and leaped up to stride to the door. When he yanked it open, Nico was on the other side, being restrained by both of Bastien's guards.

"What's going on?" Tarik demanded.

"Excuse me, Your Grace." Nico's voice, while deferential, was edged with frustration. "But there's been a most peculiar delivery."

"Deliveries are the plant manager's purview, are they not?"

"Yes, but she swears she never ordered them."

Tarik glanced back at Bastien. "Handle it for me, will you, Nico? I have a few more things to discuss with the King."

"I tried, Your Grace. But the carrier insists that he can accept no signature but yours."

"I'll come at once." If nothing else, it would delay the moment when he had to admit to his cousin that he was doomed to be a lovesick fool the rest of his days. He inclined his head at Bastien. "If you'll excuse me."

But Bastien rose gracefully. "Nonsense. I'm all agog to see what vastly important delivery demands your personal attention. Besides," he drawled, "technically this whole enterprise belongs to me. Perhaps it's time I took a more active role. Lead the way."

Tarik shook his head, but followed Nico through the lobby and the tank room to the loading dock at the back of the building, with Bastien and his guards trailing him like an impromptu royal parade.

"They're out here, Your Grace." Nico gestured to the open bay doors, and Tarik stepped outside.

There, on the concrete pad, sat a dozen oak barrels marked with the Roses Estate logo. His heart tried to climb into his throat. *Sander*. He edged forward and laid a trembling hand on the nearest barrel, the urge to laugh warring with the need to howl. Through misty eyes, he noticed the stamp on the barrel head wasn't just Roses Estate. It was entwined with the Royal Crest logo.

Bastien strolled over. "What's this?"

Tarik traced the combined logo, his throat thick. "A love letter," he whispered. He splayed his hand over the symbol and lifted his chin to meet his cousin's eyes. "Your Majesty, I have something to tell you."

Bastien's smirk was as familiar to Tarik as his own. "I imagined you might."

"And then I have a… a request. A boon to beg of you, as the operations director of your vineyards, as the Duke of Arles, as a prince of the realm—oh, and incidentally as your cousin and best friend."

"Lead the way, then." Bastien gestured for Tarik to precede him back into the winery. "I assure you, I am all ears."

CHAPTER
THIRTEEN

The next morning, Tarik paced along the grassy hilltop, an arm's length away from the border fence. Although airwaves from Roses Manor were silent as usual, the northern frequencies were busy, battering at his mind and building his headache. *I should have taken some fucking ibuprofen.*

He stopped for the hundredth time, scanning the empty vineyard to the south, and the equally empty road leading up to it. "Where are they, Bas? Have they changed their minds? Should I call—"

"Calm down." Bastien strolled over, completely at his ease as usual. "If you hadn't insisted we arrive an hour early, we could all be enjoying this highly entertaining performance in the comfort of the vineyard reception lounge." He was in full royal regalia, including his traveling crown, and with so many medals marching across his red uniform jacket that Tarik was surprised he didn't topple over from the weight. He had to be sweltering out here in the sun, but he looked as cool as if he were sipping mint tea in the shady New Palace gardens. *The fucker.*

"Do I look okay?" Tarik tugged at his collar. "Fuck, I don't look okay. I probably look parboiled. I should have worn a different suit."

"Tarik, all your suits are black, and as far as I've been able to tell, all of them are the same lightweight wool. How can you tell the difference? Although I must say..." Bastien smirked, the asshole. "The white shirt and blue tie are quite the departure from your usual funereal best."

"Shut up," Tarik muttered. He eyed the red-coated guards arrayed behind Bastien, Nico hovering to one side. "Did you have to bring the entire army with you?"

Bastien cast a glance at them, irritation flickering across his face. For the first time, Tarik wondered if being the king was something Bastien had ever wanted. He'd known from the cradle that he was destined to rule and was so very good at it. *Does he wish for a different world, a different destiny, too?*

But Bastien regained his imperturbable calm so quickly Tarik decided he'd imagined it. "Don't exaggerate, Tarik. It's barely a platoon. The protocols for two sovereigns meeting in such highly unusual circumstances are quite clear. If you'd let me arrange this in one of the neutral meeting rooms in Dulibre—"

"No! It has to be here." Tarik's gaze shifted to the east, where Eagle's Oak towered above the border. *It should be there.* But the road didn't lead up that far, nor was there room for everyone, especially if Queen Maialen brought an equivalent entourage. Not that Tarik cared who tagged along, as long as one person was in the crowd.

Sander.

Tarik resumed pacing, heading down the hill between rows of grapevines for a change of scenery. He stroked one leaf, bright green and healthy, because rain had fallen while he and Sander were marooned, and both their vineyards had recovered splendidly. He twined his finger in the tendril opposite the leaf, smiling when he remembered Sander's fascination with his curls.

"Tarik!" Bastien called, making Tarik flinch and jerk the tendril off the vine. "They're coming."

Tarik's stomach did a backflip. He stared from the broken tendril to the hilltop where his destiny could be decided with a single word, and his mouth dried. For a moment, he was tempted to run down the hill and keep running, because if he never asked the question, he would never be refused and the *potential* would always be there.

But so would regret.

So he squared his shoulders and marched up the hill in time to see a phalanx of South Abarran guards in green and gold livery lining up along the southern fence. He craned his neck, trying to see beyond that wall of muscle.

"Easy, mon cousin." Bastien's voice on the royal frequency was gentle. *"Don't rush your fences."*

Tarik bit back a snarky reply about Bastien never jumping a horse in his life, but then the guards parted to reveal Queen Maialen, Prince Zorion, Princess Enara, and Princess Katalin, all in full court splendor.

And Sander.

He was wearing a dark green jacket piped with gold and narrow black pants. Tarik had never seen him in anything other than casual clothing before—*if you don't count when he was wearing no clothing at all.* He was spectacular. Gold highlights gleamed in his hair, remnants of their time together in the sun, and his eyes were bluer than the sky arching cloudless above them.

Tarik took an unconstricted breath for the first time in more than a week.

Bastien moved to Tarik's side. "Our respectful greetings to you, Your Majesty." He inclined his head, the acknowledgement of equals. "Your Royal Highnesses." He nodded to each of the others and finally turned to Sander. "Your Grace. We thank you for agreeing to this... unconventional audience."

Queen Maialen returned Bastien's greeting, but Tarik didn't hear the words because Sander was consuming all his attention. *Does he still smell like a storm at sea? Will his skin taste of salt and rosemary? Will his—*

"Tarik," Bastien said, his tone laced with amusement. "Perhaps you and His Grace of Roses would care to chat. You may meet between the fences."

Tarik started, blinking. "Right. Yes. I would definitely care to." He scrambled gracelessly over the fence and stood twisting the grape tendril in his fingers as Sander made a more dignified approach.

Then he was *there*. No more than two hands-breadths away. *Although not close enough to smell, damn it.*

Sander smiled tentatively. "Hello."

His voice sent a shiver down Tarik's spine. "Hi. I'm so glad—" His voice thickened, and he had to swallow to clear his throat. "I've missed you."

"I've missed you, too." Sander's smile was brighter now.

"I'd take your hand, but I'm afraid the guards would tackle me."

Sander chuckled. "It's more likely yours would shoot me first and ask questions later." His smile turned wry. "Not everyone accepts my sudden miraculous redemption. I'll still be the Monster to most of them for the rest of their lives." Tarik scowled, and for some reason that made Sander laugh again. "There's my Tarik. I almost didn't recognize you without your attitude."

"People are idiots," he growled.

"Yes, I believe you've expressed that sentiment before."

"They'll see. Once they get to know you, they'll forget the Monster ever existed." He snorted. "Or else they'll assign the label to the right person. How *is* Otho, by the way?"

Sander snorted in disgust. "Residing in the *actual* Castle dungeon, still claiming to be the mastermind and refusing to name his associates. I think he fancies himself a martyr to the cause." He tilted his head, squinting up at the sky. "Not that he's ever been able to articulate what the cause is."

"I told you. A fucking terrible courier." Tarik searched Sander's face. "But what about you? Are you all right?"

"Me? I'm marvelous." *Bullshit, my darling.* The tiny stress wrinkles between Sander's eyebrows told the truth. He kept up the pretense though, leaning a little closer. "You may not have heard, but the Queen has bestowed my power moniker." Sander held out his arms. "Behold. Radioflash."

Tarik lifted both eyebrows. "Radioflash? I like it. But—"

"Apparently it's what electromagnetic pulses were called in Britain in the middle of the last century."

"How retro," Tarik said admiringly.

"What can I say?" He spread his hands, palms up. "My aunt likes her power monikers to have a bit of flair."

The sight of Sander's calluses made Tarik's dick twitch with the need to have those hands on his skin, but he held it together. Barely. "She'd *never* have come up with Deliverer."

Sander chuckled, although it held an edge of sadness. "You're right."

Tarik glanced at their mirror-image entourages, both far too close for what Tarik wanted to say. He wasn't ashamed of anything between Sander and him, but Sander's grief, Sander's feelings, were nobody's business but his own.

Tarik lifted his chin and put on his most *Your Grace*-ish attitude. "The Duke and I are stepping away. You needn't follow."

Bastien's guards shifted as if to object, but Bastien held up a hand and stilled them. The Queen simply nodded. Regally. So Tarik tilted his head and smiled at Sander. "Walk with me? I understand there's a nice view of your Manor from Eagle's Oak."

Sander's eyes darkened. *That's right.* Our *place.* Well, one of them, anyway, but the only one that was available at the moment.

The two of them strolled up the hill toward the tree, an awkward distance between them, Sander's hands clasped behind his back. Tarik continued to fiddle with the vine tendril to give him something to do with his hands, because being this close to Sander and not touching him was wrong on so many levels.

They reached the top of the knoll where the tree's branches rustled overhead, leaves dappling the sunlight on Sander's hair.

"Sander, I—"

"Tarik, I—"

Their simultaneous blurts at least broke the tension and both of them laughed, loosening the knot in Tarik's belly for the first time since he'd walked away from Sander on the beach. Sander didn't unclasp his hands, but he raised an eyebrow. "Please. You go first."

Tarik licked his lips, suddenly nervous. "I got your gift."

Sander's smile was shy, but nevertheless lit Tarik up inside. "Did you like it?"

"You know I did. It's one of the best gifts I've ever received."

"Only one of them?"

"Top three. Hands down."

Sander lifted his chin in mock disdain. "I think I'm insulted. I expected to hit the top of your personal chart. What could possibly have topped it?"

Tarik inhaled, taking his courage in both hands. "There's the incredible gift your clueless cousin Otho—"

"Second cousin."

"Stupid second cousin Otho and his coconspirators, whoever the fuck they are, gave me, all unknowing, when they kidnapped me. They thought they were trapping me with a monster, but instead they stranded me on a deserted island with the kindest, most dedicated, most wonderful man in the world."

"Tarik." Sander's voice, low and choked, arrowed straight to Tarik's heart.

"But that's only number two."

Sander's strangled laugh was a benediction. "Now I may really need to kill you for making me want to cry in front of the royal houses of both our countries, and that would be disastrous. For political reasons."

"Political. Not personal?"

Sander finally released his death clasp on his own hands so they hung relaxed at his sides. "No. Because personally, I agree. Although I'd put that at the top of my own list."

Tarik held up a finger. "Hold that thought. You haven't heard my number one pick yet."

"I'm not sure how you can top that, but go ahead."

"Well." Tarik took another deep breath. "This one might be cheating, because I don't technically have it yet. But I want it. More than anything."

"What?" Sander whispered.

"I don't know if I ever told you, but my cousin has been throwing these courtship parties for me every month or so for the last two years. Trying to set me up with an advantageous political marriage."

Sander looked as if somebody had sucker punched him. "Oh."

"He's not forcing me, you understand. I agreed to it, because I didn't think it mattered who I married, and if it benefited him and the country, I'd make it work."

"I see."

Tarik wetted his lips. "But yesterday, I told him I was wrong. I told him to cancel all future parties because it *does* matter."

"It does?" Sander whispered.

Tarik nodded slowly, never dropping his gaze from Sander's. "So much. It matters because I refuse to marry for political expediency. I will only marry for love." He smiled wryly, his stomach jittering with nerves, and held up the tendril he'd twisted into a ring. "Assuming the man I love will have me." He gulped. "Could you possibly—"

"Yes." Sander's laugh echoed across the hillside. "Of course yes. A thousand times yes." He let Tarik slip the silly tendril ring onto the third finger of his left hand and then flung his arms around Tarik, mashing their lips together in the world's most painful kiss. *Perfect.* Especially when Sander adjusted the angle and pressure and threaded his fingers through Tarik's curls in the way Tarik had come to crave.

As their kisses gentled, turning tender and careful, their bodies nestled close—*the way they should be*—Tarik realized that the noise in his head, the constant bombardment of airwave-borne messages, was still for the first time since they'd left the island.

He broke the kiss and stroked Sander's face in awe. "It's you."

Sander's forehead furrowed. "You were expecting somebody else?"

"Of course not. But my powers. The headaches. I thought it was just the island. That being surrounded by water blocked all the noise and eased the pain. But it's you. It was you all the time."

Sander drew back far enough to gaze into Tarik's eyes. "What do you mean?"

"You're like my own little island of peace. You keep the noise at bay, Sander. Will you please, *please* promise to marry me?"

"I thought we'd already covered that question, but maybe we should revisit. Is this so I can save you the cost of quality headache remedies?"

Tarik mock scowled. "No, you cheeky brat. Because I love you, of course. I think I've loved you since you nearly nailed me with that cable saw."

Sander's smile was tender. "I think I fell in love with you when you bullied me into practicing with that knife. And if that hadn't done it, the way you grounded me, encouraged me, *believed* in me, would have done it." He traced Tarik's lips with a fingertip. "Although I was probably lost the first time you called me Monster."

"No, love. We were lost *before*. But it wasn't until we disappeared onto that island that we were finally found."

"Pardon me, Your Graces." Bastien's voice carried up the hill. "This is quite the lovely show. Is there something you'd care to share with us?"

Tarik cocked his head and grinned at Sander. "Well? Do we?"

Sander gazed down at the illustrious gathering, incongruous on the sunny hillside. "I want to. I do. But will it be allowed?"

"Frankly, I don't give a fuck whether they want to allow it or not. You and me? We're definitely happening." Tarik held out his hand and breathed a sigh of pure relief when Sander took it. They strolled down the hill to join the others, but when Sander would have climbed the fence to join his aunt, Tarik tugged him closer. "Stay." Sander nodded, although his smile was a little wobbly.

Tarik bowed to Queen Maialen and Prince Zorion and then to Bastien. "Your Majesties. Your Royal Highness. His Royal Highness, Alesander Fiala, Duke of Roses, has done me the very great honor of accepting my hand in marriage."

A tiny wrinkle appeared between Queen Maialen's perfect eyebrows. "Sander, my dear, is this what you want? You're not doing it to avoid repercussions from the abduction or appease the Parliament members who are calling for retribution?"

Sander shared a smile with Tarik, squeezing his hand. "No, Your Majesty. I accepted His Grace of Arles's proposal because I love him." His smile turned to a grin. "And if he hadn't asked me, I would have asked him."

Bastien regarded Queen Maialen steadily. "Your Majesty, it has long been my opinion that it's time for the ridiculous feud between our countries to end. Unless I miss my guess, you and His Highness, Prince Zorion, feel the same."

She inclined her head. "It is so."

"Then what better way for the end to begin than with love?"

"I can't think of one, Your Majesty. Let us discuss the details."

Tarik and Sander stood hand in hand between the fences that divided their countries as their sovereigns, guards in train, strolled off down the hill. Princess Katalin shot them a cheeky grin and a thumbs-up, then hiked up her lavender chiffon skirts—revealing a sturdy pair of hiking boots—and trotted after the crowd.

Sander watched them go, his brows drawn together. "Two parliaments against us, the Ministry of Powers uncertain whether to commend me or lock me up…"

"Don't forget the paparazzi."

"And the protesters. Can't leave them out."

Tarik sighed. "It's a lot. Listen, Sander, you know I've got a temper. I'm opinionated. The stuff I hear as Wavelength can send my mood down the toilet on a regular basis. I'm not the easiest person to live with."

"You?" He widened his eyes. "Are you forgetting that I'm the Monster of Roses?"

"You're right." Tarik said with dawning wonder. "This is going to send my street cred through the roof."

Sander cradled Tarik's face in both hands. "So you won't care if it seems like the whole world is against us?"

"Are you joking?" He kissed Sander again. And twice more because he could. "This is going to be *epic*."

Her Royal Majesty Queen Maialen of South Abarra

and

His Royal Majesty King Bastien of North Abarra

are pleased to announce the marriage of

His Royal Highness The Duke of Roses

and

His Royal Highness The Duke of Arles

Wedding to be held privately at an undisclosed island location

Warning: Should anyone attempt to obtain unauthorized photographs of the ceremony, the sovereigns of neither country will be held responsible for the resulting destruction of equipment.

WHAT'S NEXT
FOR THE DUKES?

♛

A yuletide wedding brings tidings of comfort, joy... and peril.

Eighteen months ago, Tarik Jaso, Duke of Arles, would have been thrilled if Sander Fiala, Duke of Roses, sank beneath the waves along with his stupid boat.

That was then.

Now, Tarik can't wait to head out on a private sail with Sander—a sail that will culminate in a highly public, politically significant wedding. Their union will be the first one between North and South Abarran royalty in centuries. If all goes to plan, it will usher in a new era of peace and cooperation between their countries.

But as the big day approaches, their meticulous arrangements begin to fall apart. Can Sander and Tarik weather the storm of political opposition, familial objections, and outright betrayal to reach the altar at last?

The tires on the Royal Crest Bentley whispered on the newly paved street. Why did this last mile between the vineyard and Roses Manor seem to take longer than the trip from the New Palace to the vineyard? Maybe because Sander was at the other end of the road.

"*I'm telling you, Bas,*" Tarik said subvocally as the guard at the new border station recognized the car and waved it through, "*they're hiding from me on purpose.*"

"*You shock me.*" Bas's voice in Tarik's head, transmitting on their special royal frequency, was as dry as ever. "*Usually people leap at the opportunity for you to listen in on their private conversations.*"

Tarik glared out the window at the oak trees, bare of leaves now, that lined the road skirting the Roses Estate vineyard. "*You know what I mean. Unless these conspirators are smart enough to restrict communication to face-to-face meetings, landlines, or fucking Hallmark greeting cards, I should be able to pick up* something. *And let's face it, if Otho Gonzaga is a prime representative of their membership, they're not exactly rocket scientists.*"

"*Perhaps they've disbanded.*"

Tarik snorted, causing his driver to glance over his shoulder. But Jacques had been working for Tarik long enough to realize he wasn't trying to get his attention—just conducting a conversation without benefit of speaking. "*You've seen the vitriolic headlines the tabloid press has been spewing since the engagement announcement.*"

"Of course I have. I've got an entire staff of analysts who do nothing but pore through those revolting publications to sort real threats from disinformation."

"Then you need new analysts."

Bastien chuckled. "I don't know how your projected thoughts can sound sulky, but you manage."

Tarik rubbed the back of his neck, attempting to ease the headache that had grown steadily worse over the last two weeks as he'd tried unsuccessfully to track down the source of the threats to Sander's safety. *Although why I imagine I could succeed now when I haven't gotten a clue in the last year and a half, I don't know.*

He knew why he *wanted* to, of course. The tension in Sander's shoulders, the shadows in his gorgeous blue eyes when the newspapers reported yet another protest to their wedding. *Thank goodness Sander still doesn't watch televised news.* The conspiracy that resulted in their kidnapping and attempted murder was intended to ignite hostilities between their countries. Turns out all they needed for *that* was to announce the marriage of a North Abarran Royal to one from the South. Boom. Mission accomplished.

So far the hostilities had been confined to protests and political posturing by conservatives on both sides of the border, but Tarik didn't trust extremists to keep their protests non-violent. Nobody was more dangerous than someone with a *cause*.

Tarik let his head drop back against the soft leather headrest. "*I'm worried, Bas.*"

"*I know,* mon cousin." Bas's tone softened. "*And believe me, I'm taking every precaution to keep you and Sander safe.*" He chuckled. "*Holding your wedding on a private island so we have to ship all the guests in like crates of wine is one way to do it.*"

"Islands have sentimental value to Sander and me," Tarik returned huffily.

"I hardly think the luxurious resort on a billionaire's private hideaway compares in any way to the so-charming barren islet where the two of you first languished."

"I'd have been happy to go back there with only him and a couple of family members if it meant we could do without all this fuss and bother. If we'd kept things simple, we could have been married over a year ago."

"That would have been a sure way to turn public opinion against you. While the opposition factions are vocal, far more of our regular citizens are excited about the prospect of a royal wedding."

"You just want to divert their attention from the fact that you aren't getting married."

"Well, of course. Why do you think I threw myself so enthusiastically into my role as your wedding godparent?"

"You're welcome," Tarik said sourly—and out loud, judging by Jacques's rearview mirror glance.

a message from
ej

Dear Reader,

Thank you so much for reading *Duking It Out*, the first book in the new Royal Powers shared world series! I've had such a good time playing in this sandbox with the other Royal Powers authors. I hope you'll check out their books too—there's a handy list in the next page or two.

Wondering what to read next? If you're in the mood for more quirky paranormal stories, check out my screwball rom-com *Nudging Fate*, the first in my Enchanted Occasions series: it's *The Bachelor* meets *The Wedding Planner* where mythology and technology collide! Or give my Mythmatched story universe a try. It kicks off with *Cutie and the Beast*, where a cursed fae warrior turned psychologist clashes with his determined temporary office manager. As you might expect, hi-jinks ensue!

You can see all my books on my website, https://ejrussell.com, or on my Amazon author page here: https://www.amazon.com/author/ej_russell. Most are also available at Apple, Kobo, and Barnes & Noble.

Would you like exclusive content and ARC giveaways, not to mention gratuitous dance videos? Then I'd love for you to join me in Reality Optional, my Facebook fan group (https://facebook.com/groups/reality.optional). My newsletter is the place to get the latest dish on new releases, sales, and more. I promise I only send one out when I've got...well...news. You can subscribe here: https://ejrussell.com/newsletter.

All my best,
—E

Also by
ej

Paranormal Romance
Mythmatched Universe
Fae Out of Water Trilogy
Cutie and the Beast
The Druid Next Door
Bad Boy's Bard

Supernatural Selection Trilogy
Single White Incubus
Vampire With Benefits
Demon on the Down-Low

Other Mythmatched Romances
Howling on Hold
Possession in Session
Witch Under Wraps
Cursed is the Worst
The Skinny on Djinni
Assassin by Accident (part of Carnival of Mysteries)

Mythmatched Companion Stories
Rusty's Really Bad Day (free to newsletter subscribers)
Second First Date (free to newsletter subscribers)
First Flight (free to newsletter subscribers)

Quest Investigations Mysteries
Five Dead Herrings

The Hound of the Burgervilles
The Lady Under the Lake
Death on Denial

At Odds with the Gods (A Mythmatched/Purgatory
Playhouse crossover)

Art Medium Series
The Artist's Touch
Tested in Fire
Art Medium: The Complete Collection (omnibus edition)

Legend Tripping Series
Stumptown Spirits
Wolf's Clothing

Enchanted Occasions Series
Best Beast
Nudging Fate
Devouring Flame

Royal Powers Series (shared world)
Duking It Out
Duke the Hall
King's Ex

Magic Emporium Series (shared world)
Purgatory Playhouse

Monster Till Midnight

Science Fiction Romance
Sun, Moon, and Stars Series
Partnership
Principles

Historical Romance
Silent Sin

Contemporary Romance
Camera Shy
The Thomas Flair
Mystic Man
For a Good Time, Call... (A Bluewater Bay novel, with Anne
Tenino)

Christmas Kisses (holiday shorts)
The Probability of Mistletoe
An Everyday Hero
A Swants Soiree

Geeklandia Series
The Boyfriend Algorithm (M/F)
Clickbait

Writing as Nelle Heran
(traditional cozy mystery)

Crafty Sleuth Series (with C.K. Eastland)
Die Cut
Mixed Media
Found Objects (*coming soon*)

About the
Author

E.J. Russell (she/her), author of the award-winning Mythmatched paranormal romance series, writes LGBTQ+ romance and mystery in a rainbow of flavors. Count on high snark, low angst, and happy endings.

Reality? Eh, not so much.

She's married to Curmudgeonly Husband, a man who cares even less about sports than she does. Luckily, C.H. also loves to cook, or all three of their children (Lovely Daughter and Darling Sons A and B) would have survived on nothing but Cheerios, beef jerky, and Satsuma mandarins (the extent of E.J.'s culinary skill set).

E.J. also writes traditional cozy mystery as Nelle Heran. She lives in rural Oregon, enjoys visits from her wonderful adult children, and indulges in good books, red wine, and the occasional hyperbole.

News & Social Media:
Website: https://ejrussell.com
Newsletter: https://ejrussell.com/newsletter

Acknowledgements

A special thank you to Chris Cox for proposing the idea of a series about superpowered royalty. Thank you to the other authors in the Royal Powers group—Renae Kaye, Lynn Lorentz, Sara York, Jackie North, and Kenzie Blades—and to Winnie Griggs for keeping us organized.

I owe major gratitude to Meg DesCamp for editing, Fern Lee for the cover, and Leslie Copeland for general cheerleading and hand-holding.

I remain indebted to my family—Jim, Hana, Nick, Ross, and Billy—for encouragement and forbearance. Love you, guys!

And as always, thanks to you, my readers, for joining me on my writing journey. You're the reason I can continue to do what I love, and I appreciate you more than I can say.